Cyrus the Great

An Ancient Iranian King

Cyrus the Great

An Ancient Iranian King

Edited by:
Touraj Daryaee

Afshar Publishing
Santa Monica, CA 2013

Cyrus the Great
An Ancient Iranian King

Afshar Publishing
1725 Berkeley Street
Santa Monica, California 90404, USA
info@afsharpublishing.com

First Printing, August 2013

ISBN-13: 978-0-9854981-1-5

Designed by SAM Arts Design Studio, LLC.
Cover Photo: The Immortal Soldiers at Darius' palace at Susa
Back Cover: Tomb of Cyrus in 1841, after Flandin and Coste
Printed in United State of America
By
Printup Press & Graphics
Santa Monica, California
www.printup.com

TABLE OF CONTENTS

Translation of the Cyrus Cylinder

This publication has been made possible by the generous support of

www.farhang.org

Forward

Ali C. Razi

Chairman, Farhang Foundation

Cyrus the Great holds a special position in the history of civilization. His humanitarian values of freedom for all people, respect for cultural and religious diversity, and recognition of the fact that it is better to be loved than feared are remarkable attributes for any ruler. However, for someone who lived 2,600 years ago, such beliefs are truly exceptional.

Cyrus's values and ideas for governance have long inspired political thinkers and leaders of men, including the founding fathers of America, who wove these same ideals into the very constitution of the United States. Further, a copy of his cylinder hangs in the United Nations as a reminder of the first example of human rights.

So, in 2013, on the occasion of the first-ever visit of the Cyrus Cylinder to the United States—and to Los Angeles, home to the largest Iranian Diaspora community—Farhang Foundation is truly honored to present such a timely publication on this great man and his methods. We are indebted to the extraordinary group of scholars who agreed to write the essays about Cyrus the Great that comprise this volume.

Farhang Foundation's mission is to celebrate and promote Iranian art and culture for the benefit of the community-at-large, and this commemorative book does just that.

Introduction

Touraj Daryaee
University of California, Irvine

The ancient Iranians of the Achaemenid period knew about Cyrus the Great and considered him the father of the empire. Then, for reasons which are beyond the focus of this book, the Iranians lost the records of the Achaemenids and Cyrus. It took until the twentieth century for the Iranian nation to learn of this once great empire and its founder. This realization was made through the scientific endeavors of European scholars who knew the classical sources and were interested in archaeology. Gradually, scholars began to recognize Cyrus' importance and his place among the rulers of antiquity, both for the Iranian people and their collective history.

In about twenty years, Cyrus created the first great world empire of the ancient world. The lands from the Iranian Plateau to the Mediterranean were for the first time united; this would last for almost two centuries.

Cyrus' military and diplomatic skills were the cause of much success, and the echoes of his character and talent were captured in such texts as the Old Testament and *Cyropaedia*. Jews, Babylonians, and Greeks have left us laudatory accounts of Cyrus the Great, and even if not all of this is the plain truth, the unanimity of these traditions point to a very special ruler; a ruler who, before Alexander of Macedon, was able to create an empire made up of many diverse people living in relative peace and harmony. In Cyrus' empire, as long as the normal requirements of the imperial system were satisfied, religious and cultural freedoms were respected, and local traditions were kept intact. The provinces and people living in them profited greatly from the economic well-being of the Achaemenid Empire. These were the contributions of Cyrus the Great in the ancient world.

The following five essays explore the life and career of Cyrus the Great. Pierre Briant traces the life of Cyrus and how he was able to create the first great empire of antiquity from the province of Fars. I discuss the religious tolerance accorded by Cyrus to different groups and the more interesting question of the source of the king's own religious beliefs. Ali Mousavi traces the lasting importance of the monuments associated with Cyrus through Iranian history. Although the monuments and site of Pasargadae, the capital of Cyrus, was forgotten, people still paid homage to it and held it in high esteem. Matthew W. Stolper studies the Cyrus cylinder in terms of its content, aims, and motives, as well as the idea of continuity and change with other cylinders from Mesopotamia. David Stronach studies the center of Cyrus' world, namely Pasargadae. Archaeological and textual sources are brought together to give life to the location where the palace, gardens, and tomb of Cyrus were built. Finally, the recent English and Persian translation of the Cyrus cylinder are provided by Irving Finkel and Shahrokh Razmjou.

The aim of this volume is to provide a readable, yet scholarly exposition about Cyrus by experts in the field of ancient Iranian studies for the general reader. This publication was made possible through the support of the Farhang Foundation. Sam Anvari and Kate Triglia should be acknowledged for their design and editorial work. I would particularly like to thank Shazad Ghanbari in making the publication of this volume on Cyrus the Great possible. I would also like to thank Afshar Publishers for agreeing to publish this volume.

Chapter 1

Cyrus the Great

Pierre Briant
Collège de France

The Founder of the Empire

Cyrus the Great is rightly considered as the founder of the Achaemenid Persian Empire. Rising from his confined geographical base in central Fars, the new king, in the span of a few decades (559-530 BCE), took over the major kingdoms which shared the territories of the ancient Near East in the first half of the sixth century BCE: The kingdom of Lydia, including all of the western part of Asia Minor to the Hallys river; the kingdom of Media with its center around Ecbatana (Hamadan), the geographical limits of which are still a matter of debate; the Neo-Babylonian kingdom, which, under the reign of its last king, Nabonidus (556-539), covered much of the so-called Fertile Crescent (from northern Syria to the western limits of the Iranian Plateau). In addition, Cyrus undertook military expeditions within the Iranian Plateau and in Central Asia.

At the time of his death (530 BCE), only Egypt was left to be included in the Persian Empire. Cambyses II (530-522 BCE), his son and successor, accomplished the conquest of the Nile Valley.

The Achaemenid Empire, still fragile and in its formative phase, was henceforth the vastest empire that had ever been established between the Aegean Sea and Central Asia. One of the most important, and hardest, questions posed to historians about the Achaemenids is the question of how to explain the apparently sudden emergence of a new territorial power in the Near East that is characterized by its success in maintaining equilibrium of political powers.

For a long time, ancient Greek authors were the only available source of information on the Achaemenid history. Apparently, the figure of Cyrus evoked immense respect and prestige in Greece, to the point that he served as the model of the "good king," as mentioned particularly in Xenophon's *Cyropaedia*. However, it is Herodotus who gives the first and the only complete account of the life and conquests of Cyrus. In his effort to explain the origins of hostilities between the Greeks and Persians, Herodotus devoted long chapters of his book to the battles led by Cyrus. He began his account with the conquest of Lydia and the capture of Sardis by the Persian army (*Histories,* I.46-94). Before telling in the same way of Cyrus' previous expeditions against Babylon (I.177-200) and the Massagetai people of Central Asia (I.210-214), Herodotus wrote a long passage on the origins of Cyrus and his Persian kingdom, giving an account of the customs and religious and social institutions of the Persians (I.95-140). The passage is introduced as follows: "And after this our history proceeds to inquire about Cyrus, who he was that destroyed the empire of Croesus, and about the Persians, in what manner they obtained the lead of Asia."

Cyrus of Anshan

Today, we can make use of more direct and informative contemporary sources. In the Babylonian cylinder known as *the Cyrus Cylinder*, the king receives a Babylonian title ("I, Cyrus, king of the universe, mighty king, king of Babylon, etc."), but he introduces himself also

Figure 1a Sketch of the cylinder seal

in the context of his origins: "Son of Cambyses, great king, king of Anshan, grandson of Cyrus, descendant of Teispes, great king, king of Anshan." The city of Anshan is clearly situated in today's province of Fars, at the site of Tol-e Malyan, not far from the city of Parsa (Persepolis) which was subsequently founded by Darius I. According to this document, our Cyrus was then the descendent of a royal family founded by Teispes, and the son of Cambyses I, and a grandson of whom that should be considered Cyrus the First.

Furthermore, a cylinder seal (PFS 93*) [Figs. 1a and 1b], whose impression can be seen on some of the Persepolis tablets dated to the reign of Darius I, bears a fascinating inscription, written in cuneiform Elamite: "Kuraš of Anšan, son of Šešpeš [Teispes]." Here we find the first indication of the dynasty of Teispeids.

Figure 1b Impression of the cylinder seal

But, who is this Kuraš? Was he the father or uncle of our Cyrus? Nobody can identify him with certainty, but there is no doubt that he belonged to the same family that originated in Anshan, in Fars. The scene engraved on the seal is also significant; a warrior horseman is brandishing his spear, two enemies are fallen on the ground, and the third one, standing in front of him, is pierced to death. Given its style, the seal can be attributed to an artistic workshop in the court of the kingdom of Anshan in the first half of the seventh century BCE It is the place where immigrant Iranians had been interacting with the local Elamite population for centuries. As a result of this long process of ethnogenesis, the Persian people emerged, displaying both Iranian and Elamite cultural characteristics. Therefore, to that date, there does not

Figure 2 Tomb of Cyrus the Great

seem to be a question of an Achaemenid dynasty, which Darius I after his advent (522-520 BCE), glorified for its prestige and antiquity, without mentioning Cyrus as one of his ancestors. It is quite possible that the male line of Teispeids of Anshan died out with the successive demise of Cyrus II (530 BCE) and his two sons, Cambyses II and Bardiya (522 BCE). At his death, Cyrus was buried in a magnificent tomb constructed at the site of Pasargadae, in the heart of Fars [Fig. 2].

The Administration of the New Empire

Aside from the accounts offered by Greek historians, and particularly Herodotus, on the victories won over the Median and the Lydian armies, only the capture of Babylon can be reconstructed in some detail, thanks to cuneiform documents. The Cylinder testifies to the conqueror's will to establish collaboration with the political and religious elite of Babylonia: he introduces himself directly as the one who put an end to Nabonidus' exactions from the sanctuaries of Babylonia, and the one who restored these temples to their full economic and financial capacities. It is at this time that the decision was made to allow the Judean community, exiled in Babylon since Nebuchadnezzar's reign, to return to Jerusalem and to rebuild their temple there. The Cylinder does not say anything on this subject.

This information comes from Judeans themselves, particularly through the books of *Ezra* and *Nehemiah*. The *Book of Ezra* gives in quotation the text of Cyrus' decrees in this regard:

> A memorandum: In the first year of Cyrus the King, Cyrus issued a decree: 'Concerning the house of god in Jerusalem, let the house be rebuilt, the place where sacrifices are offered and burnt are brought [...]. The cost will be paid from the house of the King [...] (*Ezra* 6.2-5)

If the text is disputable, the fact in itself is undeniable. Nonetheless, Judea was not restored to the status of a kingdom. It is very probable that Judea became a province (*medinah*) ruled by a governor (*peha*) from the central power. A few years later, in 533 BCE, Judea and its adjacent territories were included in a large provincial government (*satrapy*), which covered Babylonia and the countries beyond the Euphrates (*EbirNāri*).

This simple example shows that it would be wrong to see Cyrus just as a conqueror without having a vision for organization, as this makes it clear that the satrapies existed before Darius. We know of Sardis and Daskyleion in Asia Minor, and others are known in the lands of the Iranian Plateau and Central Asia (e.g. Arachosia and Bactria). It was left to satraps to represent the great king, to implement order, and to proceed to collect taxes and human resources. The case of Gubaru in Babylonia shows the extent of the imperial administration at the time of Cyrus. Among these administrators, treasurers played an important role because each year, regional governors had to send taxes to the central government.

In Babylonia, the administration was responsible for dealing with sanctuaries, for example, with the temple of Eanna at Uruk; these sanctuaries had numerous staff, and managed extensive lands. From this time on, administrators who were directly appointed by the central government became prominent in the temple administration. These temples were in charge of paying important regular and/or exceptional contributions to the central administration. This consisted of labor provided for royal construction

Figure 3 Tomb of Cyrus 1639, after Johann Albrecht von Mandelslo

projects (digging of canals, for example) as well as of products that were to be delivered to the king and his court when they were in Babylonia. Furthermore, the satrap had to apprehend and prosecute criminals, including those that belonged to the social elite. For example, Gimillu, an oblate in charge of the livestock revenues of the Eanna, had been convicted of livestock theft and sentenced; his trial lasted several years. It is also at the time of Cyrus that the system of hatru was introduced in Babylonia: the term refers to a community that was allotted cultivated land in return for military service. These had various names such as the bow estate *(bit qasti)* or chariot estate *(bit narkabti)*, and etc. The system is particularly well-documented in the second half of the fifth century BCE, but there is no doubt that it was developed under Cyrus on the basis of pre-existing Neo-Babylonian structures.

From Cyrus to Alexander

The prestige of Cyrus remained intact among the Persians during the Achaemenid period. It is true that Darius does not mention him among his ancestors in the genealogy introduced in the Bisutun inscription. However, this does not mean that he attempted to erase Cyrus' image from the royal memory. It is possible that the inscriptions of Pasargadae in which Cyrus introduces himself as an "Achaemenid" were compiled and engraved during the reign of Darius to trace back the origin of the dynasty to Cyrus, the dynasty which the new king founded in 522 BCE after the death of Cambyses and the elimination of Bardiya, the second son of Cyrus. Also, Darius contracted marriages with Cyrus' two daughters (Atossa and Artystonè) as well as with one of Bardiya's daughters (Parmys). The names of these princesses were mentioned in the Persepolis tablets dated to the reign of Darius. It is also clear that the name of Cyrus given by Darius II to one of his sons conferred upon him a particular prestige, of which Greek texts put great emphasis.

It is ultimately through Alexander the Great that the figure of Cyrus reemerges. Accounts left by Alexander's companions presented the Macedonian conqueror as a "friend of Cyrus *(philokyros).*" The terms used for his entry in Babylon in 331 BCE closely resemble that of Cyrus, two centuries before in 539 BCE. Moreover, Alexander visited Pasargadae twice, first between January and May 330 BCE, that is between the capture and burning of the palaces at Persepolis; then in 325 BCE on his return from India before going to Persepolis and Susa. Cyrus founded Pasargadae in the heart of Persis/Fars. A formidable citadel dominates the site; there are several palaces embellished with gardens that were irrigated with canals. The most celebrated and best preserved monument is the tomb of Cyrus, to which Alexander gave particular attention. There are several Greek eyewitness descriptions of this monument, which disagree on details. Quoted by Arrian (*Anab.* VI.29.4), Aristobolus mentions that the tomb had been erected "in a royal garden *(paradeisos)*, where there were sacred trees *(alsos)* of all kinds." Aside from the contradictions between different versions, the ancient testimonies enabled the English James Morier to identify the tomb in 1811, which had been visited and illustrated for the first time in 1639 by a young German traveler, Johann Albrecht von Mandelslo (Fig. 3). Archaeological research at the site revealed traces of the gardens and irrigation canals.

At the time of his return from India in 325 BCE, Alexander was profoundly angered by learning that the tomb of Cyrus had been violated and looted:

> Alexander finds everything else removed except the sarcophagus and the divan. The robbers had even violated the body of Cyrus, for they removed the top of the sarcophagus and had thrown out the body; the sarcophagus itself they had tried to render portable, so that they might bear it away, chipping some parts away, and breaking other parts off. Not succeeding in this attempt, however, they left the sarcophagus as it was and went off" (Arrianus, *Anab.* VI.29.9).

Alexander had "the Magi, who were in charge of guarding

the tomb," arrested, but he released them soon because they remained silent under torture. The mention of these Magi led Arrian to provide complimentary information of high interest on their mission:

> Within the enclosure, and lying on the approach of the tomb itself, was a small building put up for the Magians. [...] To them was given from the King a sheep a day, and allowance of meal and wine, and a horse each month, to sacrifice to Cyrus (VI.29.7).

The information is even better understood in the context of the Persepolis tablets (dated between 492 and 458 BCE), in which the royal administration gave agricultural products and animals to be sacrificed, including those sacrifices accomplished near the tombs (šumar) of high ranked personalities of the royal family. The accounts of Alexander's companions also attest to the existence of a cult of the dead king. It is interesting to see that such a cult organized since 530 BCE still continued to be practiced two centuries later in honor of Cyrus. Then Alexander entrusted the following mission to Aristobolus:

> To put the tomb in good order again, to deposit such parts of the body as were left in the sarcophagus again, and put its lid upon it; where it was damaged, to repair it; to spread the divan with ribands,

> and to restore, just like the originals, all else that had been placed there, by way of ornament, piece by piece; to obliterate the door both by walling it up in stone and partly by covering it by clay; and then, to set on the clay the royal seal (VI.29.10).

Far from being a destroyer of Persian ancestral customs, Alexander wanted, in contrast, to demonstrate his great respect to the memory of the one who, two centuries before, had founded the Achaemenid Persian Empire; the empire that Alexander had just overtaken. Even today, the tomb of Cyrus at Pasargadae stands as a prominent "place of Achaemenid memory," which, by virtue of its unique nature, is more moving than the rock-cut tombs of his successors at Naqsh-e Rustam and Persepolis.

Bibiliography

1. Bedford, P., *Temple restoration in Early Achaemenid Judah,* Leiden, 2001.
2. Briant, P., *Bulletin d'histoireachéménide II,* Paris, 2001.
3. Briant, P., *From Cyrus to Alexander.A History of the Persian Empire,* Winona Lake (Ind.), 2002 [French 1996], en part. p. 13-106; 879-897.
4. Briant, P., *Alexander the Great and his empire,* Princeton University Press, 2010.
5. Garrison, M., "The seal of Kuraš the Anzanite, son of Šešpeš, PFS 93*: Susa—Anšan—Persepolis", in: J. Álvarez-Mon & M.B. Garrison (eds.), *Elam and Persia,* Winona Lake (Ind.), 2011, p. 375-405.
6. Jursa, M., "Taxation and service obligations in Babylonia from Nebuchadnezzar to Darius and the evidence for Darius' tax reform", in R. Rollinger—B. Truschnegg—R. Bichler (edd.), *Herodotus and the Persian Empire,* Wiesbaden, 2011, p.431-448.
7. Kuhrt, A., *The Persian empire. A corpus of sources from the Achaemenid Period,* Routledge, London, I-II, 2007, particularly I, p. 19-103.
8. Kuhrt, A., "Cyrus the Great of Persia: images and realities", in M. Heinz & M.H. Feldman (edd.), *Representations of Political Power. Case histories from Times of change and dissolving Order in the Ancient Near-East,* Winona Lake (Ind.), 2007, p. 169-191.

9. Henkelman, W., "An Elamite memorial: the *šumar* of Cambyses and Hystaspes", in W. Henkelman & A. Kuhrt (edd.), *A Persian perspective. Essays in memory of H. Sancisi-Weerdenburg* (Ach.Hist. XIII), Leiden, 2003, p. 101-172.
10. Henkelman, W., *The other Gods who are. Studies in Elamite-Iranian acculturation based on the Persepolis Fortification texts,* Leiden, 2008.
11. Henkelman, W., "Cyrus the Persian and Darius the Elamite: a case of mistaken identity", in R. Rollinger—B. Truschnegg—R. Bichler (eds.), *Herodotus and the Persian Empire,* Wiesbaden, 2011, p. 577-634.

Chapter 2

Religion of Cyrus the Great

Touraj Daryaee
University of California, Irvine

One of the most mysterious and interesting aspects of Cyrus the Great is his cooption of other religious traditions into his own religious beliefs. At the outset, it should be noted that there is much debate in regard to the ethnicity of Cyrus because of his name. Scholars are divided in this regard and some have suggested Iranian etymologies (Eilers 1974; 5-6, Schmidt 1987; 357-358), while others have provided Elamite ones (Potts 2005; 21-22, Henkelman 2008; 55). None of this can assure us of the true origins of Cyrus, as a Persian could have simply taken an Elamite name, which was the dominant culture. Cyrus was born in Anshan, one of the two important cities of the Elamite kingdom, but at a time when the Persians were ascending to power there. This suggests that Cyrus, whatever the etymology of his name might be, was born in a bicultural and perhaps a multicultural environment, where Mesopotamia and the Persian Gulf were not far away. Thus, it is not far-fetched to assume that already in his youth he had been exposed to other religious traditions, and that this must have had an impact on his dealings with other religious communities.

It is also important that in his encounter with the Mesopotamian and Jewish people, Cyrus is mentioned as a benevolent ruler who is amiable to the religion of his subjects. This is markedly different from the policy of the previous ruler in Mesopotamia. Cyrus, in both the Babylonian and Jewish texts, acts as a restorer of a chaotic situation, where the rightful god(s) and men are dissatisfied, while the unrighteous men are in charge. Then, Cyrus is chosen by the god(s) and evokes the love of the god(s) of each city and people. For example, in the city of Uruk, a short stamped brick reads: "(Cyrus) loves Esangil and Ezida" (Kuhrt 2007; 74), while another inscription from the city of Ur mentions that he "returned the gods to their shrines" (Khurt 2007; 75). Thus, love, restoration and being chosen appear to run through the texts produced, especially in Mesopotamia.

Another theme that the Babylonian and Biblical traditions associate Cyrus with is his peaceful nature and his establishment of peace in the realm. Of course, this may be later propaganda by the scribes written under Persian rule, but it is noteworthy that we do not get any alternative traditions, and so we must conclude that there is some truth to what was written.

An Akkadian text from Babylon or Sippar, condemning the preceding ruler of Babylon, Nabounides, for his carelessness in regard to proper ceremonies and religious practices, states that "he (Cyrus) declared peace for them" and that he provided the proper sacrifices for the gods and even increased the amount for the sacrifice (Kuhrt 2007; 78). In this way, Cyrus becomes the chosen instrument of the gods who have been neglected by the ill reputed ruler. In a similar fashion, Cyrus is seen by the Jewish God as his supporter: "Behold my servant, whom I uphold, my chosen one in whom I delight" (*Isaiah* 42.1).

In the Old Testament, Cyrus achieves unrivaled status, and Yahweh calls onto Cyrus in such a fashion:

> "who says of Cyrus, 'He is my shepherd and will accomplish all that I please; he will say of Jerusalem, "Let it be rebuilt," and of the temple, "Let its foundations be laid This is what the LORD says to his anointed, to Cyrus, whose right hand I take hold" (*Isaiah* 44.28-45.1)

It is in *Ezra* that we find the same theme of restoring the temple of god which we find in the Mesopotamian documents mentioned above. Cyrus' decree stated "Let the temple be rebuilt as a place to present sacrifices, and let its foundations be laid" (*Ezra* 6.2-5). Again, the restoration of sacrifices is mentioned. In *Ezra* we also come across the notion that while the previous ruler, here Nebuchadnezzar, had taken things out of the temple, it is Cyrus who will restore things back, as the Bible states "returned to their places" (*Ezra* 6.5).

This idea is important not merely for propaganda purposes, which Cyrus was able to achieve in a myriad of traditions, but because, I would contend, of a very Iranian idea. The theme of "putting back into order what has become undone" is also an idea associated with Ahuramazda. Ahuramazda, or the Wise Lord, is the representative of Order in the cosmos, while Angra Mainyu is the representative of Disorder/Lie (Skjærvø 2011; 10). If we read these texts within the Iranian ideological framework, we see a clear Iranian/ Mazdean view of the king restoring Order (Avestan *Asha*/ Old Persian *Arta*) on earth, as the agent of Ahuramazda. Consequently, the unruly kings of the old (Nebuchadnezzar, Nabonidus, etc.) become agents of Disorder/Lie, the Evil Spirit or Angra Mainyu. After all, Nabonidus had come to power in Babylon as a result of a coup and Cyrus provides a narrative where he is shown as attempting to restore order. These actions of Cyrus are strongly similar to those of Darius I's Behistun inscription where the king attempts to explain the disorder that had been caused after the death of Cambyses and the accession of an imposter, Gaumata. Darius, in taking on Gaumata and deposing him, in effect destroyed the agent of Angra Mainyu and restored Order to the empire.

The Cyrus Cylinder is the best example of presenting the conquering king as the restorer of Order and the harbinger of peace to an otherwise chaotic world. According to the cylinder, what had taken place before Cyrus was the forsaking of the New Year festival with its proper rituals, which caused much dissatisfaction, not only for men, but also for the gods. Of course, Marduk, the most important of the Mesopotamian gods, just like Yahweh, chose Cyrus to reinstate what had gone wrong. The parallels between Isaiah and the Cyrus Cylinder are striking: "he (Marduk) took him by the hand: Cyrus, king of Anshan" (CC line 12) is strongly reminiscent of Isaiah 44.28-45.1 "Cyrus whom he (Yahweh) has taken by the hand." (Kuhrt 2007; 83)

Thus, whether it is Yahweh, Marduk or other gods, Cyrus' action appears to be consistent according to both Jewish and Mesopotamian tradition. The practical function of such restoration was, first and foremost, to appease the local priesthood and local elites. By working with them, Cyrus was able to co-opt them into the new imperial structure that he was building. Cyrus the Great portrayed himself as someone within these traditions (Briant 2002; 79).

Cyrus the Great's Religion

Since Cyrus appears as the one chosen by the local gods of Mesopotamia and the Jewish god, his own religious beliefs become a matter of intense interest.

There are arguments for both his Iranian/Mazdean and non-Iranian beliefs and practices. It should be noted that most of the accounts and reports about him were written long after his death. Furthermore, we are not sure about the state of Mazdaism and its connection with the early Achaemenid rulers (Kellens 2000; 27-28). Xenophon, writing almost a century later, mentions that Cyrus was "educated in the Persian manner," (*Cyropaedia* I, 2.2) and that he followed the magi's instructions (*Cyropaedia* 4.5.14). Thus his education appears to have been connected with the Mazdean tradition, as the magi were a Median tribe who constituted the priestly class. The magi memorized and recited the sacred hymns, performed the proper sacrifices, and tended to the sacred fires.

It is also important to note that the most well-known daughter of Cyrus was named Atossa (Avestan Hutaosā), which is a name associated with the Mazdean tradition. According to the sacred Mazdean hagiography, it was Kavi Vishtaspa (Persian *Kay Goshtasb*) who accepted and made current the religious ideas of Zarathushtra (Zoroaster). The name of Kavi Vishtaspa's wife is mentioned as Hutaosā, which suggests that Cyrus may have been aware of this ancient tradition.

More important is the evidence from his royal residence, Pasargadae, where his palace and royal tomb stands. Here, there is circumstantial evidence that may suggest not only an Iranian practice, but also a

Mazdean tradition at work. There are stone fire-holders which can be traced to the Mazdean cult of the fire (Stronach, *Pasargadae,* Oxford, 1978, p. 141). Cyrus' tomb is also interesting in that while the model is certainly inspired by Western Asia, the body of the king was kept from touching the sacred earth, in line with the Mazdean tradition. More importantly, there once stood a carved image of a flower over the entrance of the tomb, (Stronach 1971; 155 and figure 7 in this volume by Stronach) which is now lost. This flower was similar to that of the lotus which Mithra stands over at the Taq-e Bustan from the Sasanian period. Hence, one can speculate that Cyrus had a connection with Mithra, the important pre-Zoroastrian deity, who was later brought into the Mazdean fold (Duchesne-Guillemin 1974; 7).

The lotus is not the only evidence pointing to Cyrus the Great honoring Mithra. We are also told that after Cyrus' death, regular sacrificial services were performed at the tomb by the magi. The sacrifices included the following:

> "The king used to give them a sheep a day, a fixed amount of meal and wine, and a horse each month to sacrifice to Cyrus" (Ctesias VI.29.7)

These commodities are similar to that of the Sasanian period in the third century CE, when Shapur I offered similar commodities for the souls of his royal family according to the Ka'be-ye Zardosht inscription (Panaino 2005; 114). Thus, whether the practice is Mazdean in origin or not, we see that it was continued into the Sasanian period and that it had long existed among the Persians in the province of Fars. More importantly in the passage from Ctesias, there is the mention of a horse sacrifice. The order by Cyrus' son, Cambyses, to sacrifice a horse for his father, is clearly part of the Indo-Iranian practice of *aśvamedha*. In the *Cyropaedia*, there are references to royal parades by Cyrus, where a white horse and fire are mentioned. The horse sacrifice is explained in the following manner (*Cyropaedia* VIII.3.12):

> "After the oxen came horses, an offering to the Sun, then a white chariot with a golden yoke, hung with garlands and dedicated to Zeus, and after that the white chariot of the Sun, wreathed like the one before it, and then a third chariot, the horses of which were caparisoned with scarlet trappings, and behind walked men carrying fire upon a mighty hearth."

The story is indeed part of a ritual procession, where the chariot was dedicated to the Sun. The Sun here is clearly Mithra (Briant 2002; 96 : Swennen 2004; p. 170). Mithra is one of the great gods (Old Persian *baga*) of the Indo-Iranians who, while not mentioned in the early Achaemenid inscriptions, makes his appearance there during the rule of Artaxerxes II at the end of the fifth century BCE. There are other classical authors who mention the large number of horses the Persians demanded of their subjects (Strabo XI.14.9 "20,000 horses for the feast of Mithra"), as well as specifically mentioning sacred white horses during Cyrus' conquest of Babylon (Herodotus I.189 : Briant 2002; 96).

Mithra was considered one of the important gods (Avestan *yazata*), to whom one of the longest hymns in the Mazdean sacred hymns, the *Avesta*, are dedicated. However, it should be remembered that Mithra as a deity was important before the development of Mazdaism in the Indian and the Iranian worlds. Mithra, whose primary function is related to contracts and oaths (Schmidt 1978; 351), is also associated with the sun and martial qualities. These qualities of Mithra, especially in connection with the sun, is similar to what classical sources report on Cyrus. On the other hand, the Avestan hymn dedicated to Mithra also has commonalities with the ritual parade of Cyrus in the *Cyropaedia* (Swennen 2004; 174-175).

To conclude, Cyrus the Great clearly brought an unprecedented vision of religious tolerance to the region. We can only guess as to the main reason for his allowance of the Jews and Babylonians to freely practice their religion, but the fact is that he did so.

For this reason, not only the Mesopotamian tradition, but also in the living Jewish religion, Cyrus would be fondly remembered and honored for centuries. In contrast, we know far less about his own personal religious beliefs, but the circumstantial evidence clearly point to Iranian practices. His name can only give us minor clues as to the place where he was living, but his actions provide a much better example of the manner in which this king ruled in the ancient Near East and over the Iranian Empire of the Achaemenids.

Trilingual Old Persian, Babylonian and Elamite inscription above the figure:

"I, Cyrus the king, an Achaemenid"

Charles Texier, Description de l'Arménie, la Perse et la Mésopotamie, Paris, 1852.

Bibliography

1. Briant, P., *From Cyrus to Alexander. A History of the Persian Empire,* Eisenbrauns, 2002.
2. Duchesene-Guillemin, J., "Le dieu de Cyrus," *Acta Iranica* 3, 1974, Leiden, pp. 11-24.
3. Eilers, W., "The name of Cyrus," *Acta Iranica 3*, Leiden, pp. 3-10.
4. Henkelman, W., *The Other Gods Who Are: Studies in Elamite-Iranian Acculturation Based on the Persepolis Fortification Texts,* Leiden, 2008.
5. Kellens, J., *Essays on Zarathustra and Zoroastrianism,* Mazda Publishers, 2000.
6. Kuhrt, A., *The Persian Empire. A Corpus of Sources from the Achaemenid Period,* vol. I, Routledge, 2007.
7. Panaino, A., "Sheep, Weat, and Wine: An Achaemenian Antecedent of the Sasanian Sacrifices *pad ruwān,*" BAI 19, 2005, pp. 111-118.
8. Potts, D., "Cyrus the Great and the Kingdom of Anshan," *Birth of the Persian Empire,* eds. V. Sarkhosh Curtis & S. Stewart, I.B. Tauris, 2005, pp. 7-28.
9. Schmidt, H-P., "Indo-Iranian Mitra Studies: The State of the Central Problem," in *Études Mithriaques,* Acta Iranica 17, Leiden, 1978, pp. 345-93.
10. Schmidt, H-P., "An Indo-Iranian etymological kaleidoscope," *Festschrift for Henry Hoenigswalded.* G. Cardona, Ars linguistica 15, 1987, 355-362.

11. Skjærvø, P.O., *The Spirit of Zoroastrianism,* Yale, 2001.
12. Stronach, D. "A circular symbol on the tomb of Cyrus," Iran 9, 1971, pp. 155-158.
13. D. Stronach, D. *Pasargadae,* Oxford, 1978.
14. Swennen, Ph., *D'Indra à Tištrya. Portrait et évolution du cheval sacré dans les mythes indo-iraniens anciens,* Paris, 2004.

Chapter 3

Pilgrimage to Pasargadae

A Brief History of the Site from the Fall of the Achaemenids to the Early Twentieth Century

Ali Mousavi
Los Angeles County Museum of Art

Neither the Macedonian conquest nor the Arab invasion of Persia put an end to the long life of Achaemenid capital cities such as Pasargadae and Persepolis. These are the monuments that have played symbolic roles as emblems of identity, representing historical legacies and crucial moments of achievement along the stream of human civilization. After the fall of the Persian Empire in 330 BCE, the monuments at Pasargadae, the capital city of Cyrus the Great, avoided the disastrous fate of Persepolis by both the virtue of the highly respected personality of Cyrus and its geographical situation.

Classical authors tell us that Alexander paid homage to Cyrus by visiting his tomb, built in a royal park at Pasargadae. The undoubtedly apocryphal Greek inscription on the Tomb of Cyrus mentioned in Alexander's tradition is a particularly interesting example of the Greek world's admiration for Cyrus, as well as the Greek interpretation of foreign ways of life. However, Alexander's visit was not without self-serving motivation. Alexander's quest for legitimacy was an insurmountable problem, stemming from the impossibility of relating himself by blood to the Achaemenid family. His visit to Pasargadae was an act of last resort to gain the support of the Persian population. The same historians of Alexander also inform us that the Macedonian conqueror went to Pasargadae to appropriate the royal treasures housed at the old capital city (Arrian, *Anabasis of Alexander*, III, 18, 10). The Greco-Macedonian conquerors did not leave much at the site except for the third century BCE occupation of the large citadel, the ruins of which have been found at Tall-e Takht located near the royal city. In fact, little is known about the history of the site during the one thousand years that separate the end of the Achaemenid Empire and the Muslim conquest of Fars in the seventh century.

The Sasanian kings, themselves native to Fars and probably descendants of the Achaemenid line, used Istakhr as a royal residence and regional center. They remained attracted by the ruins of Persepolis only 5 kilometers away and so magnificently located against the mountains. They did not seem to have a particular interest in the site of Pasargadae, despite the fact that a few, insignificant rock-cut remains confined to an outlying northeastern area of the site have survived from that period. In one instance, one of the late Sasanian visitors of Pasargadae carved on the stone the record of his visit, which is nothing but an enigmatic plan of the ruined citadel of Tall-e Takht.

Pasargadae in Medieval Times

The true names of the builders of such impressive Achaemenid monuments were gradually lost in the course of time. In such circumstances, most of the impressive ruined monuments of the Achaemenid period became places of fascination, evoking a glorious past of spiritual and mythological associations, rather than literal historical recollections. Eventually, they came to be ascribed to two popularly mythical historical figures. The first of these was Jamshid, the mythical, paramount hero-king of ancient Iran, whose name has frequently been mentioned in Ferdowsi's *Shahnama (Book of Kings)*; the second was Solomon, who in the Koran was known as a ruler of extraordinary power and wisdom.

In the twelfth century, Ibn Balkhi, the author of the famous *Farsnamah*, briefly mentioned the monumental tomb as being located in a meadow that "lay in the neighborhood of the Tomb of Solomon's mother... He describes it as "a square built house of stone which no one dare look inside, for fear lest he should become blind." Hamdullah Mostowfi, in his *Nuzhat al-Qolub* uses the same information to describe the building. With his rationalism and critical mind, Hamdullah did not follow the strange ideas that had been put forward by Muhammad ibn Mahmud Hamadani, in his *Ajā'eb-Nāmeh (Book of Wonders)* of c.590 H./1194 CE. Hamadani considered the monuments of Pasargadae and Persepolis to be among the works that monsters must have made, so incredible were the engineering feats they represented. Such an opinion was also shared by the celebrated historian of the Timurid period, Hafiz Abru. In his *Chronicles (Tarikh-e Hafez-e Abru)*, he describes the marghzar or meadow of Kalan as being near mashhad-e madar-e Suleiman, the tomb of the mother of Solomon, and attributed such a finely cut monument, including those located near Istakhr (Persepolis) to the genii (monsters) who were subservient to Solomon.

For one hundred twenty years, Fars was ruled by the Salghurid family of Atabaks (543-686 H./ 1148-1287 CE), who were tributaries first of the Saljuqs, then of the Mongols. In this way, they saved Fars from the ravages of the Mongol armies. The province seems to have enjoyed moderate prosperity, especially during the reign of Izz al-Din Sa'd, from whom the celebrated poet, Sa'di, derived his *takhallus* or *nom de plume.* At Pasargadae, the same ruler changed the compound surrounding the tomb of Cyrus into a mosque, and his name is recorded in several places, giving the date of 620 H./ 1223 CE. Inside the building, in the tomb chamber, the presence of a shallow prayer- niche or mihrab, and elaborately carved compass on one of the tiers of the base clearly show that the tomb served as the central part of the medieval mosque. A hoard of gold coins from the same dynasty was found at a spot to the northwest of the tomb of Cyrus when the area was being levelled in April 1971. In the introduction to his *Gulestan*, Sa'di uses the expression of "heir to the Kingdom of Solomon" among the titles attributed to the Atabak Abu Bakr, son of Sa'd. There are inscriptions of this dynasty engraved on stone blocks taken from the Achaemenid palaces at Pasargadae. Almost all of these inscriptions mention the name of the Salghurid ruler as the heir to the realm of Jam and Solomon; the two personalities were often considered one.

After a period of conflict, the region was under the suzerainty of Shah Shuja (r. 759–786 H./1358–1384 CE), another ruler of high cultural standards and a great patron of the arts, whose reign was jubilantly greeted by the celebrated Iranian poet Hafiz. Shah Shuja constructed a large building, probably a residence or caravanserai, in the proximity of the tomb of Cyrus at Pasargadae, and a number of coins and inscriptions dated to his reign were found in the excavation of the building in 1949.

European Travelers and Pasargadae

Giosafat Barbaro, a Venetian ambassador and merchant, who visited the site in 1474, writes that the monument was known as the "Tomb of Solomon's Mother." Given its isolated location on the side of the major route that connected Shiraz to Isfahan, the ruins at Pasargadae did not attract the notable European travelers of the seventeenth century such as Figueroa, Tavernier, and Chardin, with two exceptions. The Roman Pietro Della Valle, who must have passed by the ruins in 1621, only makes an allusion to the presence of a tomb at Pasargadae attributed to Solomon's mother. The German ambassador, Johann Albrecht von Madelslo, who went to see Persepolis and Pasargadae in 1638, visited the site and described the tomb of Cyrus as being "in a little chapel, built of white marble, upon a high square of free stonework." His engraving of the tomb, produced most probably after sketches made at the spot, is the only picture of the monument before the far more accurate illustrations of the nineteenth century. As for the attribution of the tomb to Solomon's mother, the Carmelite Father of Shiraz told the young traveller that the monument was the "sepulchre of the mother of Shah Suleiman, the fourteenth caliph." For the Dutchmen, John Struys and Cornelis de Bruijn, the tomb was a place of "feminine pilgrimage." Interestingly, this tradition seems to be still in practice today.

Pasargadae in the 19th and 20th Centuries

The downfall of the Safavid kingdom in 1722 interrupted European exploratory visits for some decades. Pasargadae, due to its remote situation, did not figure in the itinerary of at least two notable travelers of the eighteenth century, the German Carsten Niebuhr and the English William Francklin, who limited their visits to the ruins at Persepolis. The advent of the Qajars in 1779 re-established political stability in Iran. Both of the first two rulers of this dynasty, Aqa-Muhammad-Khan and Fath-Ali Shah, had a strong sense of Iranian identity. Fath-Ali Shah, who was first the governor of Fars, must have seen the glorious ruins at Persepolis and Naqsh-e Rustam, the source of inspiration for his own rock-reliefs at Shiraz and Rey. The Europeans' travels to Persia were intensified because of the Napoleonic wars in Europe and the Russo-Persian conflicts between 1804 and 1828. A series of British and French diplomatic missions were sent to Persia with the aim of seeking alliances for an ultimate intervention of Persia in case of any threat to India.

The British accounts of the ruins at Persepolis, namely those left by William Ouseley, James Morier, and Robert Ker Porter, make use of both the preceding travelers' writings and their own meticulous observations and research. Ouseley draws largely on historians and geographers of Islamic Iran, but also uses Greek and Latin sources. Ouseley's description of the site and its remains was without doubt the most conspicuous account of Pasargadae hitherto published in the West. He mentions the Takht-e Madar-e Suleiman (the Throne of Solomon's Mother) known as Tall-e Takht, the Divan-Khanhe or the Achaemenid Audience hall (Palace S) with its singly standing column, the Zendan or Prison of Solomon that resembled so perfectly that at Naqsh-e Rustam, before described as seemingly having been erected for the same purpose (whatever it may have been) and during the same period, the medieval caravanserai, and finally, the monument known as the Tomb of Solomon's Mother. Equally important is the account left by James Morier, the secretary of the diplomatic mission, who is the first author to draw attention to the fact that the so-called Tomb of the Mother of Solomon corresponds to the monument described by the classical authors, such as Arrian and Strabo, as the Tomb of Cyrus the Great.

Robert Ker Porter, an Englishman in the service of the Russian Empire, was the first visitor to Pasargadae to refer to the ruins by this name. Both Ker Porter and the French architect Charles Texier published drawings of the winged figure and the trilingual inscription which once surmounted it, which were only superseded by the publication of the most elaborate work of Flandin and Coste in 1851, *Voyage en Perse* (Figures 1 & 2).

The honor of documenting the ruins by means of the most fascinating technical invention of the century went to Colonel Luigi Pesce, an Italian infantry officer from Naples, who took the first photographs of the ruins at Persepolis and Pasargadae in 1857. These pictures preceded those taken later by Stolze in the 1870s and 1880s.

Lord Curzon's contribution to the study of Pasargadae is the culminating point, in which he attempted a thorough study of the ruins and a comprehensive synthesis of all knowledge of the site acquired to date.

Figure 1 Tomb of Cyrus in 1841, after Flandin and Coste

He devoted some twenty pages of his book, *Persia and the Persian Question* (London, 1892, vol. 2), to the description and interpretation of the remains at Pasargadae, examining all the relevant textual evidence coupled with his own sharp observations. In his opinion, the edifice known as the tomb of Solomon's Mother provided "a further point of absolute correspondence" with classical accounts. It is interesting to note that Curzon's work interested the German Assyriologist, Friedrich Weissbach, who in an article posed the following questions: "Where did Pasargadae lie? Do the ruins of Murghab correspond to that antique place? How did the tomb of Cyrus look? What was the meaning of the "Tomb of the mother of Solomon"? and to which ruler do the inscriptions of Murghab belong?" Of these questions, he finally found

Figure 2 The ruined monument known as Zendan-e Suleiman in 1841, after Flandin and Coste

an answer for: the Tomb of Solomon's Mother is not the tomb of Cyrus; the monument known as Zendan corresponds better to the textual evidence left by classical writers, and finally, the CMa inscription in cuneiform is from the time of Cyrus the Younger (the fifth century BCE), and the relief of the Winged Figure was erected by his mother, Parysatis, in reminiscence of her son.

Ernst Herzfeld's excavation of the major Achaemenid ruins of Fars, in particular those at Pasargadae and Persepolis, from 1928 to 1934, opened an unprecedented era of scientific research, the history of which has been given particular attention in the past twenty years.

Bibliography

1. Curzon, G. N., *Persia and the Persian Question,* London, 1892, vol. 2.
2. Gabriel, A., *Die Erforschung Persiens,* Vienna, 1952.
3. Ouseley, W., *Travels in Various Countries of the East, more particularly Persia,* London, 1821, vol. 2.
4. Mousavi, A., *Persepolis. Discovery and Afterlife of a World Wonder,* Berlin, 2012.
5. Sami, A., *Pasargadae,* Shiraz, 1956.
6. Sancisi-Weerdenburg, H. "Through travellers' eyes: the Persian monuments as seen by European visitors", in *Through Travellers' Eyes. European Travellers on the Iranian Monuments,* AchHist VII, H. Sancisi-Weerdenburg and J. W. Drijvers (eds.), Leiden, 1991, pp. 1-35.
7. Stronach, D., *Pasaragadae,* Oxford, 1978.
8. Stronach, D.,"Pasargadae after Cyrus the Great: different paradigms for different times", *The Gift of Persian Culture: Its Continuity and Influence in History, Reza Ali Khazeni Memorial Lectures in Iranian Studies* 1, P. J. Chelkowski (ed.), Salt Lake City, Utah, 2011, 71-94.
9. Weissbach, F., "Das Grab des Cyrus und die Inschriften von Murghab," *Zeitschrift der Deutschen Morgenländischen Gesellschaft,* vol. 48, 1894, pp. 653-665.

Chapter 4

The Form, Language and Contents of the Cyrus Cylinder

Matthew W. Stolper
University of Chicago

The Babylonian scribes who composed the Cyrus Cylinder drew on a millennium-long tradition of Babylonian and Assyrian royal building inscriptions. In such texts, kings not only commemorated the construction or reconstruction of temples, palaces, fortifications, canals and other public works, but also used the occasion to memorialize their names, their genealogies and titles, their attributes, the gods' sponsorship of their reigns, and sometimes their deeds. The objects that carried the texts were often included in the structure or foundations of the buildings that they commemorated, with the expectation that future rulers and their scribes would rediscover them, recognize them, and respect them. Thus, these documents express an ancient sense of what a modern person might call *history*, by embodying and sometimes citing a deep past and by expressing an expectation of an indefinite future. The information that the rulers chose to convey informs, but also constrains, later knowledge of the Mesopotamian past, including the historical understanding of modern observers.

The barrel-shaped clay "Cylinder" resembles the objects that carried many Babylonian royal inscriptions from the reigns of the Neo-Assyrian and Neo-Babylonian kings, beginning in the eighth century BCE. The Cyrus Cylinder is one of the last known examples of these. Its text is laid out in 45 lines that run all the way across the long axis. In this respect, it differs from the inscribed cylinders of the Neo-Babylonian kings who immediately preceded Cyrus, which usually have texts laid out in two parallel columns running around the circumference. Instead, it resembles its older counterparts that commemorate Neo-Assyrian kings; the resemblance may be deliberate.

The Cyrus Cylinder was discovered in 1879 in the area of Babylon where Esagil, the great temple of Marduk, had stood. Only recently, parts of another copy of the text of the Cylinder were identified on two fragments of a single clay tablet in the Babylon collections of the British Museum, the remains of an archival copy of the inscription, which can be found here: *(http://www.britishmuseum.org/research/search_the_collection_database/search_results).*

The forms of the cuneiform signs that record the text resemble contemporary Neo-Babylonian forms in current use, not the ornamental, archaizing sign forms that some inscriptions of the Neo-Babylonian kings prefer. The language of the text is a version of the Babylonian dialect of Akkadian called Standard Babylonian. It was the language of literature and learning, scholarship and science, as well as of royal inscriptions, both in Assyria and in Babylonia. By comparison with contemporary letters—that is, with examples of the language in which people actually communicated with each other—it is marked by exalted vocabulary, arch and stilted grammatical forms and archaizing usages. The sound of Cyrus's message was grand and old.

The main message, the conqueror's portrayal of himself as a restorer of order, is a venerable royal theme. The compositional elements of this portrayal—from the opening temporal clause that sets the scene to the closing prayer for divine blessing—belong to a well-established repertoire. Such exalted language arrayed in these familiar forms minimized novelty for ancient readers or hearers, even where modern observers recognize an announcement of historic change.

Contents

As the newly discovered tablet fragments confirm, the text of the Cylinder begins (lines 1-10) from the point of view of Marduk, the god of Babylon and the supreme god of the Babylonian pantheon, who observes with divine anger the condition of Babylonia under its Babylonian king. Many details are lost to damage, but the passage refers, in charged language, to the construction and endowment of a sacrilegious shrine, to the abrogation of proper support for Marduk's temple and cult, an assault on reverence for the supreme god, to ruinous impositions on the people, and to anger and abandonment by the other gods, whose images had been brought to Babylon and kept there. The name of the wicked Babylonian king responsible, Nabonidus (ruled 555-539 BCE), is lost. The passage apparently implicates his son and regent in these sins, foreshadowing Cyrus's later association of his own son, Cambyses, with his righteous restoration of order.

As the text continues, (10-12) still told from Marduk's point of view, the god's anger relents. He contemplates the ruined sanctuaries (again foreshadowing Cyrus's restoration), and the near-death condition of the people of "Sumer and Akkad" (a traditional term for Babylonia). The field of view widens as he surveys all lands and looks closely for a righteous king. He finds Cyrus (12-13), king of Anshan (the ancient Elamite capital of the territory that was now Persia), takes him by the hand, calls him to be supreme ruler, and subjugates Media and the mountain territories that bordered Babylonia (again using old literary terms, not contemporary political names for these regions).

Pleased with Cyrus's accomplishments, Marduk orders Cyrus to go to Babylon (14-15). Now the view narrows and descends from heavenly oversight to earthly participation (15-17). Marduk escorts Cyrus, walking at his side "like a friend and companion," while his vast army marches beside him under arms. Marduk brings Cyrus into the very heart of Babylon, the district called Shuanna, where the royal palace and the temple of Marduk were, "without conflict or battle." He hands over the impious Babylonian king Nabonidus (of whom no more is said). The people of Babylon and of Babylonia, their leaders and their governors (again using old terms without contemporary political currency), do homage to him, delighted to praise him as a savior (18-19).

The narrative point of view has shifted in stages from Marduk's oversight of Babylonia and his wider survey of all the lands, to Cyrus's ascent in western Iran and his progress into Babylonia, and then to Cyrus enthroned in the midst of Babylon. Then, the perspective changes from Marduk's to Cyrus's own. The remainder of the text is given as Cyrus's own words, beginning with "I am Cyrus ..." (20).

Cyrus identifies himself in three ways: first (20), in political terms, with a series of Mesopotamian royal epithets, some especially favored by Assyrian kings, asserting universal dominion, both over Babylonia and over the entire world; second (21) in decidedly non-Babylonian genealogical and geographical terms, as the descendant of three generations of kings of Anshan, making him the "perpetual seed of kingship" as Babylonian rulers must be; third (22), in religious terms, as the protégé of the Babylonian gods Bēl (Marduk) and Nabû.

The next lines echo, in Cyrus's voice, essential elements of the impersonal narrative in the first part of the text. Cyrus elaborates on his peaceable entry into Babylon (22, 24), and the consequent relief of Babylonia from anxiety, oppression, and exhaustion (24-26). He repeats that he brought this about as an agent of Marduk (23). He adds that he now made the palace of Babylon his own royal seat (23).

Just as Marduk had earlier taken pleasure in Cyrus's ascendancy in Iran (14), so now, Cyrus says, Marduk was pleased with these good deeds in Babylonia. Marduk rewarded the deeds with blessings on Cyrus and his son Cambyses (the righteous counterpart of the wicked Babylonian prince-regent [3]) and on his conquering army (26-28). And just as the people and leaders of Babylonia kissed Cyrus's feet (18), now he tells of enthroned rulers from everywhere, from the Mediterranean to the Persian Gulf, and tent-dwelling kings of the west country, who brought tribute and kissed his feet in Babylon (28-30).

Then, in a sharp shift to geographical specificity, Cyrus speaks of towns and territories in Assyria, northern Babylonia, the land along the Diyala River and east of the Tigris River as far as Susa in Khuzestan, areas that had lain between Babylonia proper to the west and Media and Persia to the east. He says that he renovated their dilapidated sanctuaries, brought their gods back and restored their populations, using imagery of ingathering and resettlement that had been customary for expressing the re-establishment of peaceful order since the days of Hammurabi of Babylon (30-32). He rectifies the impiety with which Nabonidus had enraged the gods of Babylonia (9-10) by returning them to their shrines (33-34). He prays that the restored gods will repay this good deed by speaking well of him before the great gods of Babylon, Bēl (Marduk) and Nabû (his son), calling for blessings on Cyrus himself, and on Cambyses, his son (34-36).

In the final damaged lines, Cyrus tells of his efforts to carry out the duties of a Babylonian ruler as a supporter of the temple cult and as a builder. He describes an oddly modest increase in daily offerings of poultry (presumably for Marduk, 37). He says that he planned to strengthen the main fortification wall of Babylon, as if to reiterate that Babylon was not a conquered enemy citadel but his own political seat (38). He takes credit for completing an unfinished canal embankment with baked bricks and bitumen (39-41).

He describes fitting a structure (perhaps the temple of Marduk) with doors of cedar clad with bronze, along with their thresholds and fittings (42-43). And he says that in the course of the work, he discovered and restored an inscription in the name of the Assyrian king Assurbanipal (43-44), just as the building inscriptions of his foe, Nabonidus, had spoken of finding documents of ancient kings of Babylonia. Cyrus's text ends with a prayer to Marduk for the gift of a long life, an enduring reign and an eternal memory (44-45).

Composition and Audience

The royal inscriptions of Babylonian and Assyrian kings sometimes refer to "experts" or "scholars" whom the rulers consulted about building projects, about identifying old inscriptions and preparing new ones. Scribes recopied old inscriptions, and as the recently discovered tablet fragments show, this happened to the text of the Cyrus Cylinder. The name of the scribe who made the copy, Qishti-Marduk, is preserved. The name of the person who composed the original text is not.

The composer's work shows an "expert's" knowledge of vocabulary, epithets, formulas and tropes, compositional elements that might convey gravity rather than freshness. Behind this pompous surface, his work also shows concern for careful, elegant structure. The beginning of the text is a genre-crossing innovation: the opening temporal clause that establishes the scene and occasion is a feature found in earlier inscriptions on stelae displayed in the open, but not those on cylinders to be placed in the foundations of buildings. The absence of Cyrus from the opening lines is extraordinary in a royal inscription, where the focal topic is the king, but it creates a different kind of focus through anticipation. The initial description of Nabonidus's wickedness has its nearest counterpart in a stele inscription of Nabonidus himself that describes the devastation of Babylon by the Assyrians generations earlier. The cross-references and change of voice between the first and second parts of Cyrus's text enliven the message that Cyrus's reign was the fulfillment of Marduk's will more effectively than mere assertion and repetition. The shifting points of view, from heaven to earth, from Iran to Babylon, and from Babylon outward, convey a quality of performance.

For whom was this editorial craft intended? Cyrus himself had to be satisfied, of course, and the future ruler who might find the object, as Cyrus had found an inscription of Assurbanipal. The simplistic idea that such documents were intended *only* for the king, the gods, and posterity is contradicted by many examples of archived or displayed copies of inscriptions of Neo-Assyrian and Neo-Babylonian kings, inscriptions of Cyrus's Achaemenid successors, and now by the tablet fragments with Qishti-Marduk's copy of this text. The composer had an audience in view, yet the scope of the audience, the means of presenting the text to it, and the process transmitting the text to later scholars like Qishti-Marduk, remain matters of speculation, uncertainty and disagreement

Empire and Succession

The text depicts Cyrus and his army as peaceful occupiers of Babylon, ignoring their defeat of the Babylonian army in battles a few months earlier. With Cyrus's statements that established his residence in the royal palace of Babylon, took control over the Babylonian people and their governors, and took tribute from rulers of the west, he is portrayed both as the rightful king of Babylonia and as the acknowledged ruler of Babylonia's tributary empire across the Euphrates. A reader or hearer could suppose that Babylon remained the capital and center of the empire and was to become the center of Cyrus's larger empire.

In several passages, Cyrus associates himself with his son, Cambyses. The nearest parallels for these passages are in inscriptions of Cyrus's despised predecessor, Nabonidus, which sometimes call similarly for blessings on his son Belshazzar. They are tantamount to designating an heir-apparent, highlighting one of the great problems of all ancient monarchies, the problem of dynastic succession. Other Babylonian documents offer glimpses of what was involved. A Babylonian Chronicle tells that Cyrus formally installed his son Cambyses at the annual New Year's ritual at the beginning of his reign. Date formulas on legal tablets from the following year, the first full regnal year of Cyrus, refer to Cambyses as "king of Babylon," and Cyrus as "king of (all) the Lands," preserving, at least in name, a kingdom of Babylonia within the greater Persian Empire. This was a short-lived expedient. After a year, Cambyses's name ceased to appear in dates. Shortly afterwards, legal and administrative texts began to refer to satraps with the title "governor of Babylon and Across-the-River (i.e., the Euphrates)." Their province was nominally coterminous with the conquered Babylonian empire and they governed it from Babylon, but as Persian governors, not as Babylonian kings. Eight years after Cyrus entered Babylon, Cambyses succeeded him without trouble as the single ruler of the whole empire and its parts. In the parlance of Babylonian legal texts, he was known as "king of Babylon and king of (all) the Lands," ruling from 529 to 522 BCE.

The Cyrus Cylinder and Later Babylonian Inscriptions

The text of the Cylinder describes the restoration of an existing order, with Babylon at its center, but once Babylonia was incorporated into an empire that encompassed a whole continent, many things were bound to change, including Babylonian royal inscriptions. Two other short inscriptions of Cyrus have been found at sites in southern Babylonia, both stamped on bricks that were used in royal building projects. One, from Ur, portrays him, like the Cylinder text, as a benign foreign conqueror, in terms similar to the Cylinder; it calls him "king of Anshan," says that the gods gave him control of all lands, and that he settled "the land" (Babylonia) in peace. The other, from Uruk, simply characterizes him as the mighty king, lover of the temples Esagil (temple of Marduk) and Ezida (temple of Nabû), things that might have been said of any Babylonian ruler.

No comparable documents of Cyrus's Persian successors have come to light in Babylonia. As far as it is known, they did not sponsor and commemorate the reconstruction of temples and palaces in customary Babylonian forms. From the reign of Darius I on, the inscriptions of the Achaemenid kings at the palaces of Persepolis and Susa, on the cliff face at Bisutun in western Iran, and elsewhere regularly included versions in Babylonian language, alongside versions in Elamite and Old Persian. A few fragments of such trilingual inscriptions were found in the palace complex at Babylon.

In form and content, these later Achaemenid inscriptions were very different from older Mesopotamian royal inscriptions and from the text of the Cyrus Cylinder. Their aims did not include an assurance of Mesopotamian continuity. Even so, in the longest and most elaborate of them, the great inscription of Darius I at Bisutun, the Babylonian version sometimes departs from the Old Persian and Elamite versions in ways that were meant for a particular, Babylonian audience. In fact, in a fragmentary Babylonian edition of this text on a damaged stone monument in Babylon itself, the god who chooses, guides, and supports King Darius, called Ahuramazda in the main edition, is instead called Bēl, allowing a Babylonian reader or hearer to suppose that Marduk was meant—that Marduk, who guided Cyrus, also guided Darius.

The tradition to which the Cyrus Cylinder belonged was not entirely forgotten. After the Seleucid successors of Alexander the Great had established control of Babylonia, Antiochus I (ruled 281-261 BCE) left an inscription on a similar barrel-shaped clay cylinder. It is laid out like older Babylonian examples in two parallel columns and written in archaizing sign forms. It commemorates the reconstruction of the Ezida, the temple of Nabû at Borsippa, near Babylon. As in the Cyrus Cylinder, the prayers for blessings associate the king with his son and successor (but unlike the Cyrus Cylinder, also with his wife). The Antiochus Cylinder is the latest known document of this kind.

Chapter 5

Cyrus and Pasargadae

David Stronach
University of California, Berkeley

The memorable mountain-ringed site of Pasargadae, which stands 1900 m above sea level and some 50 km to the northeast of Persepolis as the crow flies, is inextricably linked to the name of its celebrated founder, Cyrus the Great (559-530 BCE). Since only a limited number of inscriptions from Mesopotamia can be securely attributed to Cyrus, the ruins of this majestic site (Fig. 1) may be said to represent a significant, additional source of information about the tastes and standards of this singular monarch. In this concise introduction to the capital and last resting place of Cyrus, I will attempt to provide a brief description of the initial excavations that were carried out at the site; a short description of most of the main monuments; and certain comments on the history of the fourfold garden (or *chaharbagh*) -- a form of Persian garden that may conceivably owe its origin to Cyrus' personal interest in gardens.

Excavations at the site

To begin with, it has to be stated that the site of Pasargadae benefited greatly from the fact that its original excavator was the gifted archaeologist, Ernst Herzfeld (1879-1948). When Herzfeld embarked on his first studies at Pasargadae at the beginning of the twentieth century the identity of the site was still not known for certain. This was also at a time when the study of Achaemenid art and architecture was very much in its infancy. But Herzfeld was at once aware of the exceptional importance of Pasargadae; and I think it is true to say that, despite the fact that his archaeological interests stretched from prehistoric times down to the Islamic era, problems and questions related to the interpretation of the monuments at Pasargadae continued to engage him for the rest of his life.

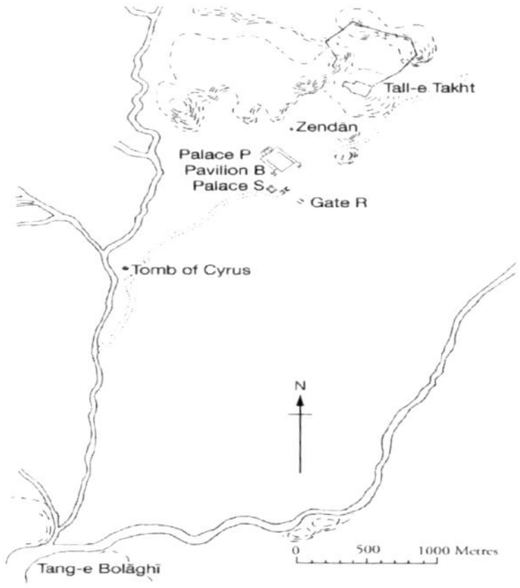

Figure 1 Sketch plan of Pasargadae.

Two cuneiform inscriptions were still in plain sight at Pasargadae at the time of Herzfeld's first visit in 1905. Each was an example of the same trilingual "CMa inscription", written in Old Persian, Elamite and Akkadian, and Herzfeld instantly grasped the fact that the intended reading of the text was "I, Cyrus, the King, an Achaemenid (built this monument)". Accordingly, he was able to state, without equivocation, that the mysteriously named ruins situated in the immediate vicinity of the so-called Ghabr-e Madar-e Soleiman or "Tomb of the Mother of Solomon" in the modern Dasht-e Morghab or "Plain of the Water-bird" were those of the long-lost capital of Cyrus the Great (Herzfeld 1908).

It is also of interest that already at the time of his first visit to the site Herzfeld clearly understood that the one surviving relief in the monumental gate structure was a winged genius in the age-old tradition of Mesopotamian (and most especially Neo-Assyrian) apotropaic doorway figures (Fig. 2). That is to say that he never subscribed to a palpably mistaken belief that the winged figure, with its divine headdress and its supernatural wings, could represent a portrait of Cyrus. (Cf. Sarre and Herzfeld 1910: 159-160.)

In view of all that was accomplished during Herzfeld's single four-week season of formal excavations in 1928, one can only marvel that the entire staff of the expedition consisted of Herzfeld himself and

Friedrich Krefter, a twenty-five year-old architect! Needless to say, Herzfeld's description of his excavations was cursory by modern standards (Herzfeld 1929: 1-16). Nonetheless, he quickly grasped the main characteristics of this spacious site. In particular, he recognized that most of the principal structures shared – in an entirely new departure for the architecture of ancient Iran – a common orientation.

The next excavations to be conducted at Pasargadae were those directed by Ali Sami on behalf of the

Figure 2 Drawing of the winged figure from the Gate of Cyrus.

Iranian Archaeological Service. A very considerable debt is owed to this pioneer Iranian archaeologist, who excavated at Pasargadae from 1949 to 1955. During the years in question he carried out an extensive program of work, clearing the area surrounding the tomb of Cyrus; exposing and planning a number of early Islamic structures in the vicinity of the tomb; finding the first traces of the site's principal garden; and adding significant details to the still far-from-completely recorded plans of Pasargadae's three distinct palatial buildings (Sami 1971). In the meantime the latest excavations to take place at Pasargadae were those conducted by the present writer, on behalf of the British Institute of Persian Studies, from 1961 to 1963. This work led to the detailed publication of most of Pasargadae's main monuments (Stronach 1978) as well as to the recovery of still further elements of the plan of the main garden with its finely carved

Figure 12 A recreation of the Palace of Cyrus and the adjacent chaharbagh or fourfold garden. (After Rezaeian 2013: pl. 63.)

stone water channels and stone water basins (Figs. 1, 10 and 12).

The location of Pasargadae

The fact that it took so long to discover the correct location of Pasargadae can probably be attributed to two principal factors. First, its true identity came to be concealed behind the names of mythical historical figures (cf. Mousavi, this volume) that would appear to have been ascribed to certain of the monuments in early medieval times, well after the original associations of the site had long been forgotten. And secondly, instead of being located somewhere in the core region of modern Fars in say, the immediate vicinity of Persepolis, the site proved to have been situated in one of the more elevated, northerly plains of Fars, albeit on the line of the immemorial highway that linked Fars to the central and northern parts of Iran.

A plausible explanation for this surprising location is contained in the writings of Strabo, the Greek geographer and historian of the first century BCE. In Strabo's account we learn that "Cyrus held Pasargadae in honor because he there conquered Astyages the Mede in his last battle, transferred to himself the empire of Asia, founded a city, and constructed a palace as a memorial to his victory" (Strabo 15.3.8). If this account is to be believed (and I see no compelling reason why it should not be), Cyrus elected to build his tomb and the other major monuments of his capital on the site of the battle, in 550 BCE, in which he defeated the last Median king, Astyages. This crucial event guaranteed the continued independence of the Persians and paved the way for Cyrus' subsequent, far-flung exploits.

Providentially, Cyrus' next major campaign proved to be against Croesus, the king of Lydia, (who, in keeping with Astyages, would also appear to have initiated hostilities). In the end Cyrus prevailed, not least because of his rare capacity for doing the unexpected. Thus Croesus' supposedly impenetrable acropolis at Sardis fell to Cyrus' arms in November 547 after a siege of only 14 days – and, from that moment forwards, the many highly skilled Ionian and Lydian stone masons whom Croesus had employed in many separate ways (cf. Stronach 2008: 153-154), were suddenly at Cyrus' sole disposal.

Through a rather fortunate combination of circumstances, in other words, Cyrus suddenly found himself with the means to erect a lasting monument to his reign that could be characterized by state-of-the-art planning and state-of-the-art stone architecture. As he must have at once appreciated, this was an opportunity not to be missed.

Construction at Pasargadae

As far as it is still possible to determine, Cyrus' major buildings were not only situated according to the provisions of a single master plan, but they were probably very largely founded within a few years of each other. The one individual structure that most visibly supports the case for something in the nature of a fifteen-year program of construction from c. 546 BCE down to the moment of Cyrus' death in 530 BCE is the great stone Terrace that juts out from the west side of the Tall-e Takht (Fig. 3), near the northern limit of the site. The construction of this dominant feature (which was probably intended to support the western end of a planned but never-realized residential palace) was a massive and time-consuming task that still remained far from totally finished at the time of Cyrus' death. Indeed, the roughly protruding central bosses that appear on so many of the unfinished ashlar blocks persuaded Roman Ghirshman that the whole platform had to antedate Cyrus' more refined constructions in the adjacent plain and he chose to ascribe the entire monument to Cambyses I, the father of Cyrus.

However, as Carl Nylander (1970) was able to demonstrate, the true intended finish was nothing less than highly sophisticated. It called for finely drafted margins and delicate point stippling on the slightly raised central panels on the face of each stone block (Fig. 4) – a style of surface dressing that is otherwise attested in western Asia Minor, especially in the middle years of the 6th century BCE Nylander's timely observation calls to mind,

Figure 3 The huge stone Terrace that protrudes from the west side of the Tall-e Takht.

Figure 4 A detail from the west façade of the stone Terrace. Note the slightly raised central panels and neatly drafted edges that are characteristic of each of the few, fully finished ashlars.

in fact, the testimony of Cyrus' near successor, Darius the Great (522-486 BCE), who relates (in his famous "foundation inscription" from Susa) that "the stone-cutters who wrought the stone, those were Ionians and Sardians" (Kent 1953: 144).

The tomb of Cyrus

The setting of the tomb is masterly. It stands apart from all the other major monuments, where it dominates the southern half of the Morghab plain (Fig. 1). With its massive stonework and smooth surfaces, relieved by no more than a minimum of decorative detail, the tomb creates an indelible impression of dignity, simplicity and strength. In design it combines two distinct elements: a high plinth composed of six receding tiers and a modest, gabled tomb chamber (Fig. 5).

While the tomb stands out as a further structure that offers an unusually direct reflection of the presence of skilled architects and masons from Lydia and Ionia, it has to be stressed that no matter how much the fabric of the tomb can be said to owe to the canons of one or another architectural style, it is necessary to presume that this iconic monument met the prescriptions of Cyrus himself. Beyond everything else, it was a structure that had to meet the standards, choices and beliefs of the founder of Pasargadae.

In March 1969 the remains of a protruding rosette that would seem to have escaped any prior explicit notice were found on the apex of the triangular gable above the low doorway of the tomb (Stronach 1971). Whether or not the now incomplete rosette at the apex of the entrance gable (Figs. 6 and 7) was originally intended to carry religious connotations or was never intended to be anything more than a skeuomorphic echo of the decorative end of a wooden ridge pole may never be known. All that can be said for certain is that no exactly similar rosette is known from any other context.

Figure 5 The tomb of Cyrus seen from the west in 1961. The column drums were erected in the first quarter of the 13th century CE when the Atabak ruler, Izz al-Din Sa'd, chose to make the tomb – revered at the time as the "Tomb of the Mother of Solomon" -- the focal point of a congregational mosque.

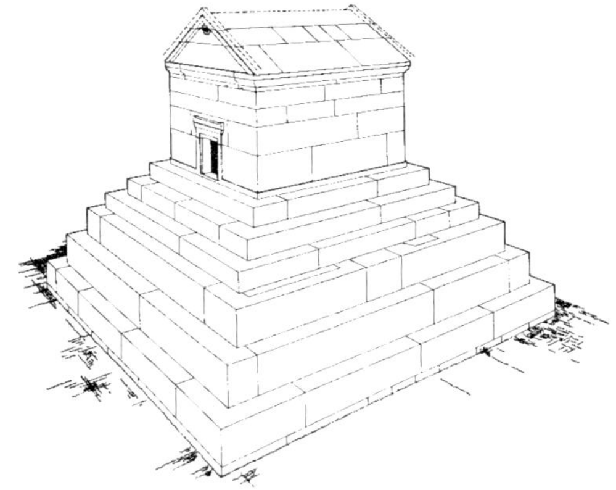

Figure 6 Drawing of the tomb of Cyrus. The top course of the roof and the missing portion of the rosette at the apex of the entrance gable are each restored, as is the ground level that was probably associated with the completed monument. (After Stronach 1978: fig. 21.)

Figure 7 A reconstruction of the probable original appearance of the rosette on the tomb of Cyrus. (After Roaf 1983: fig. 147.)

The Gate of Cyrus

Formerly known as Gate R (or "the Palace with the Relief"), the Gate of Cyrus (Fig. 1) is a further significant structure in the history of Iranian architecture. As a freestanding, formal gate it served, at least in broad terms, as a prototype for the Gate of Darius at Susa (Perrot 2010) and for the Gate of Xerxes at Persepolis (Schmidt 1953). Its freestanding character is particularly unusual in that every city gate in the ancient Near East down to the time of Cyrus was invariably embedded in a towering perimeter wall. In the present case, in other words, Cyrus appears to have been making a statement to the effect that his gleaming capital city had no need for such fixed, fortified features: features that had always characterized earlier capitals of standing, such as Nineveh and Babylon. But while the freestanding gates at Susa and Persepolis each possessed four columns within a square columned hall (in keeping with Darius' preference for square-shaped rooms), the Gate of Cyrus possessed a rectangular hall with two rows of four tall stone columns (Fig. 8). This was already a familiar plan for reception halls in the competent mud-brick and wood architecture of neighboring Media (cf. Stronach and Roaf 2007; Gopnik and Rothman 2011), and this suggests that similar plans were already attested in Fars or were borrowed, very possibly from the region of Media, following Cyrus' annexation of that more northerly kingdom.

In borrowing (and adapting) various aspects of the best available building techniques and protective images that he knew of, Cyrus turned, as we have already seen, to the recently "orphaned", but still powerful protective imagery of Assyria. Thus, in searching for appropriate apotropaic images to guard the two main and two side doorways of his sixteen-meter-high gate, he settled on two pairs of giant winged colossi to guard the two opposed main doorways – a solution that later came to be repeated in Xerxes' "Gate of All Lands" at Persepolis (Schmidt 1953). At the same time two pairs of protective anthropomorphic figures undoubtedly occupied the stone jambs of the side doorways and, as we know from the one surviving example (Fig. 2), these latter figures faced inwards not

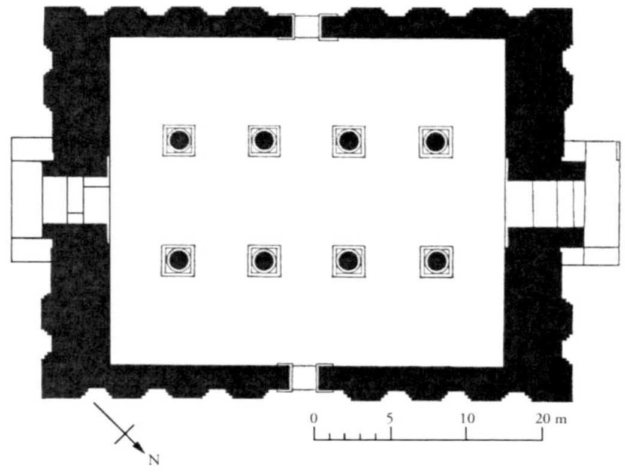

Figure 8 The Gate of Cyrus. A reconstruction of the plan, showing the two rows of four columns that were used to support the roof of the hall.

outwards in order, it must be assumed, to prevent malevolent forces from making their way down the main axis of the gate into the site as a whole.

Today we know that, on leaving the gate and progressing towards the next major destination, the Audience Hall, visitors would have suddenly come in full view of a man-made trapezoidal lake (Benech, Boucharlat and Gondet 2012). Finally, after visitors seeking an audience with the king had crossed a bridge located at the narrow, southern end of this distinctive stretch of water (Fig. 1), they would presumably have been conducted to an appropriate station within the tall eight-columned Audience Hall (a structure also known to archaeologists as Palace S).

The Audience Hall

This structure (Fig. 8) was one of two imposing and innovative palaces that Cyrus introduced at Pasargadae. It can also be said to have served as one of the more important prototypes for the consummate audience hall of the reign of Darius: the uniformly tall, square-shaped Apadana (such as was defined in Old Persian inscriptions as being "of stone in its columns").

As a still rather experimental structure, the design of the Audience Hall draws on an interesting mixture of Iranian and non-Iranian architectural traits. It echoed such earlier phenomena, for example, as the tall eight-columned halls of Iron Age Iran (in which the main hall, with two rows of four wooden columns, was flanked on occasion by a low columned portico that marked the only entrance). It also echoes the kind of corner chambers that were once used to strengthen the design of early first millennium "manor houses" in central western Iran. (Cf. Dyson 1989; Goff 1969.) Its principal glory, however, consisted of its soaring white stone columns. Such columns were complemented, moreover, by black stone column bases and animal-headed capitals. Column capitals of this novel form (with magnificent addorsed animal heads) may well have been an Iranian invention; and, as it happens, the earliest known examples of the type were found in the Audience Hall during Herzfeld's excavations in 1928 (Herzfeld 1941).

Figure 9 A recreation of the Audience Hall and its immediate environs, seen from the south. Pavilion B stands in the background. (After Rezaeian 2013: pl. 77.)

The plan of the Audience Hall also bears witness to something else that was novel in the long history of Iranian architecture: namely a bold new four-sided design that was marked by deep inviting porticoes (with double rows of columns) on each side of the building (Fig. 9). As Boardman (2000) has pointed out, such a four-sided plan appears to draw on the design of the early Ionic dipteral temple (even if temples of this kind were characterized by continuous flanking colonnades that rose to the full height of the structure).

Certain of the protective doorway reliefs in the Audience Hall proved to be closely modeled on late Assyrian prototypes. Indeed, it may be no accident that Cyrus chose to copy guardian figures of a type that the formidable Assyrian ruler, Sennacherib (704-681 BC), had used to adorn his own "palace without rival" at Nineveh. It should only be added that Assyrian-related protective images were probably already well known in western Iran (where there had been much interaction with the Assyrians from at least the end of the 8th century BC onwards). Accordingly, it would be wrong to think such supernatural protective beings were only employed for what they would have meant to contemporary visitors from say, the region of Mesopotamia. They would probably also have spelled out messages of power and legitimacy to members of Cyrus' extended "home constituency" throughout western Iran (Stronach 1997).

The Palace of Cyrus

Even though this inner palace – also known as "Palace P" – was almost certainly part of Cyrus' carefully considered master plan, it stands out as one of the few structures at Pasargadae that Cyrus never came close to completing. Each of the thirty stone columns (disposed in five rows of six columns in the finely paved

Figure 11 The Palace of Cyrus. An incomplete stone column from the southwestern end of the hall. Note especially the horizontally fluted torus base that stands on a two-stepped plinth composed of black and white stone elements.

central hall) appears, in fact, to have been only one drum high at the time that Cyrus died (Fig. 11).

Nevertheless all the individual stone elements that were completed by 530 BCE can be said to underscore the extreme care that was originally lavished on this building. For this reason alone I am inclined to think that this particular palace was the one structure that Cyrus regarded as being his ultimate "personal palace".

In a curious way the subsequent history of this same building does much to affirm this conclusion. That is to say that when Darius decided that he should erect numerous copies of the above-mentioned CMa inscription in each of Cyrus' three palatial structures, he also clearly decided to make his most striking effort to link Cyrus to his own Achaemenid line while completing the fabric of the Palace of Cyrus. To this end, he erected handsome bas-reliefs of Cyrus in each of the palace's two main doorways. And he duly labeled each of these images with the same third-person CMc text reading "Cyrus, the great king, an Achaemenid".

It is quite remarkable that we owe the completion of the Palace of Cyrus, not to Cyrus' son and successor, Cambyses II (530-522BCE), but to the efforts of Darius I (even if we know that the latter used wood and brightly painted plaster, rather than stone, to complete the thirty columns of the hall.) In addition, there are sound grounds (based on closely dated chisel marks) for thinking that the stone elements of the innermost garden at Pasargadae were themselves unfinished in certain places at the time of Cyrus' death – and that this arresting creation also owes its completion to the care and attention of Darius.

The fourfold garden

Until a little over twenty years ago it was generally believed that the Persian fourfold garden – the *chaharbagh* – probably only dated back to the Safavid period when gardens of this kind were known to have existed in Isfahan. At the same time there was always a strong likelihood that gardens of this type could have enjoyed a much longer history (cf. Stronach 1989). In this connection attention has not seldom been drawn to an intriguing encounter between Cyrus the Younger (d. 401 BCE), who might be supposed to have shared some of the tastes and interests of his famous namesake, and the Spartan admiral, Lysander (cf. Stronach 1994). In Xenophon's account (Xen. *Oec.* 4.20-5) this second son of Darius II is proud to point out certain trees (some of which he had planted with his own hands) on his estates near Sardis. And Lysander, in turn, is reported to have marveled at the trees "finely and evenly planted" and at the way everything was "exact and arranged at right angles".

Even though I tried for several years to relate this story in some useful way to the evidence "on the ground" in the innermost garden at Pasargadae, I did not make much progress until I began to work with a draftsman on a preliminary reconstruction of the garden. In written instructions I asked the draftsman to arrange the trees in straight rows within the two successive rectangular spaces that the various water channels seemed to define as the overall space of the garden. Then, when the drawing arrived, I was dismayed

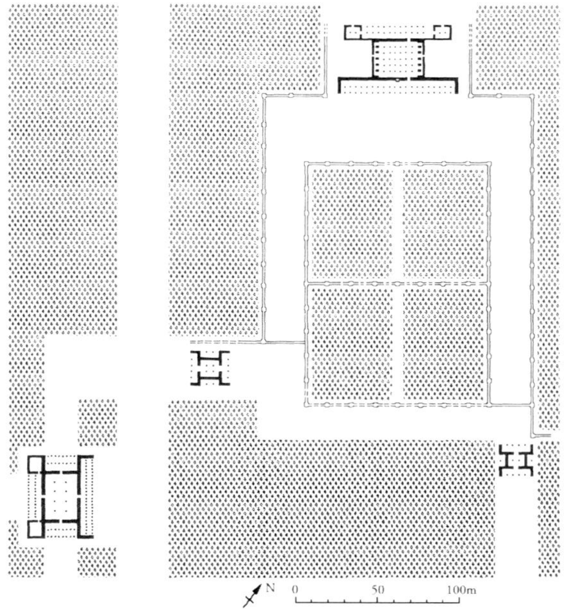

Figure 10 Plan of the Palace of Cyrus and the adjacent fourfold garden. Pavilion B, situated to the left of the garden, would appear to have stood on the route that connected the Audience Hall to the Palace of Cyrus.

to find that a long line of bushes had been placed directly in front of the external throne seat of the king at the mid-point of the portico. As far as the monarch's enjoyment of his garden was concerned, this clearly made no sense at all! Then the situation suddenly became plain: I realized that the king would have insisted on an uninterrupted line of sight down the long axis of his choice garden – and that once this "view of power" was accommodated (as in Figure 10) we would no longer have a somewhat uninteresting design composed of two large rectangles, but we would have the essence of the design of a fourfold garden with four distinct *parterres*.

I might just add that, if the principal characteristics of this kind of palatial garden were then subsequently preserved – not least in Iran, but also in many other lands – for many centuries, this circumstance can hardly be attributed to the simplicity and elegance of Cyrus' original "garden blueprint" alone. Such a phenomenon calls, in short, for a consideration of other factors as well. While an association with the name and repute of Cyrus the Great may have sufficed to give a garden of this fourfold character a special cachet for not a few generations, such a situation cannot have continued indefinitely. It is perhaps possible to propose, therefore, that over a very much longer period of time a garden of this kind came to be viewed as a time-honored symbol of legitimate rule.

Bibliography

1. Benech, C., Boucharlat, R. and Gondet, S., "Organisation et aménagement de l'espace à Pasargades: Reconnaissances archéologiques de surface 2003-2008", Arta 2012.003: 1-37.
2. Boardman, J., *Persia and the West: An Archaeological Investigation of the Genesis of Achaemenid Art*, London, 2000.
3. Dyson, R.H., "The Iron Age architecture at Hasanlu: An essay". *Expedition* 31, nos. 2-3: 107-127.
4. Goff, C., "Excavations at Baba Jan 1967: Second preliminary report", *Iran* 7, 1969: 115-130.
5. Gopnik, H. and Rothman, M.S., *On the High Road: The History of Godin Tepe, Iran,* Costa Mesa, California, 2011.
6. Herzfeld, E., "Pasargadae. Untersuchungen zur persischen Archäologie", *Klio* 8,1908: 1-68.
7. Herzfeld, E., "Bericht über die Ausgrabungen von Pasargadae 1928", *Archäologische Mitteilungen aus Iran* 1, 1929: 1-16.
8. Herzfeld, E., *Iran in the Ancient East,* London and New York, 1941.
9. Kent, R.G., *Old Persian: Grammar, Texts, Lexicon,* 2nd ed., New Haven, Connecticut, 1953.
10. Nylander, C., *Ionians in Pasargadae: Studies in Old Persian Architecture,* Uppsala, 1970.
11. Perrot, J., *Le palais de Darius à Suse,* Paris, 2010.

12. Rezaeian, F., *Recreating Pasargadae,* Toronto, 2013.
13. Roaf, M., *Sculptures and Sculptors at Persepolis, Iran* 21, 1983.
14. Sami, A., *Pasargadae*, Shiraz, 1971.
15. Sarre, F. and Herzfeld, E., *Iranische Felsreliefs*, Berlin, 1910.
16. Schmidt, E.F., *Persepolis* 1, Chicago, 1953.
17. Stronach, D.,"A circular symbol on the tomb of Cyrus", *Iran* 9, 1971:155-158.
18. Stronach, D., *Pasargadae A Report on the Excavations Conducted by the British Instititute of Persian Studies from 1961 to 1963*, Oxford, 1978.
19. Stronach, D., "The royal garden at Pasargadae: Evolution and legacy". in *Archaeologia Iranica et Orientalis: Miscellanea in Honorem Louis Vanden Berghe* 1, L. De Meyer and E. Haerinck (eds.), Ghent, 1989.
20. Stronach, D. "The garden as a political statement: Some case studies from the Near East in the first millennium BC", *Bulletin of the Asia Institute* 4, 1990: 171-180.
21. Stronach, D., "Anshan and Parsa: Early Achaemenid history, art and architecture on the Iranian Plateau", in *Mesopotamia and Iran in the Persian Period: Conquest and Imperialism 539-331 BC*, J. Curtis, (ed.), London: 35-53.

22. Stronach, D., "The building program of Cyrus the Great at Pasargadae and the date of the fall of Sardis", in *Ancient Greece and Ancient Iran: Cross-Cultural Encounters*, S.M.R. Darbandi and A. Zournatzi (eds.), Athens: 149-173.
23. Stronach, D. and Roaf, M., *Nush-i Jan* I. *The Major Buildings of the Median Settlement, Leuven.*

Chapter 6

Translation of the Cyrus Cylinder

Irving Finkel,
Department of the Middle East
The British Museum

1. [When ... Mar]duk, king of the whole of heaven and earth, the .... who, in his ..., lays waste his.......
2. [..] broad? in intelligence, ... who inspects (?) the wor]ld quarters (regions)
3. [..] his [first] born (=Belshazzar), a low person, was put in charge of his country,
4. but [.. ....] he set [a (...) counter]feit over them.
5. He ma[de] a counterfeit of Esagil, [and ....]... for Ur and the rest of the cult-cities.
6. Rites inappropriate to them, [impure] fo[od-offerings ....] disrespectful [...] were daily gabbled, and, as an insult,

7. he brought the daily offerings to a halt; he inter[fered with the rites and] instituted [.......] within the sanctuaries. In his mind, reverential fear of Marduk, king of the gods, came to an end.
8. He did yet more evil to his city every day; ... his [people ....], he brought ruin on them all by a yoke without relief.
9. Enlil-of-the-gods became extremely angry at their complaints, and [...] their territory. The gods who lived within them left their shrines,
10. angry that he had made (them) enter into Shuanna (Babylon). Ex[alted Marduk, Enlil-of-the-Go]ds, relented. He changed his mind about all the settlements whose sanctuaries were in ruins,
11. and the population of the land of Sumer and Akkad who had become like corpses, and took pity on them. He inspected and checked all the countries,
12. seeking for the upright king of his choice. He took the hand of Cyrus, king of the city of Anshan, and called him by his name, proclaiming him aloud for the kingship over all of everything.
13. He made the land of Guti and all the Median troops prostrate themselves at his feet, while he shepherded in justice and righteousness the black-headed people
14. whom he had put under his care. Marduk, the great lord, who nurtures his people, saw with

pleasure his fine deeds and true heart,

15. and ordered that he should go to Babylon. He had him take the road to Tintir (Babylon), and, like a friend and companion, he walked at his side.
16. His vast troops whose number, like the water in a river, could not be counted, were marching fully-armed at his side.
17. He had him enter without fighting or battle right into Shuanna; he saved his city Babylon from hardship. He handed over to him Nabonidus, the king who did not fear him.
18. All the people of Tintir, of all Sumer and Akkad, nobles and governors, bowed down before him and kissed his feet, rejoicing over his kingship and their faces shone.
19. The lord through whose help all were rescued from death and who saved them all from distress and hardship, they blessed him sweetly and praised his name.
20. I am Cyrus, king of the universe, the great king, the powerful king, king of Babylon, king of Sumer and Akkad, king of the four quarters of the world,
21. son of Cambyses, the great king, king of the city of Anshan, grandson of Cyrus, the great king, ki[ng of the ci]ty of Anshan, descendant of Teispes, the great king, king of the city of Anshan,
22. the perpetual seed of kingship, whose reign Bel (Marduk)and Nabu love, and with whose kingship,

to their joy, they concern themselves. When I went as harbinger of peace i[nt]o Babylon

23. I founded my sovereign residence within the palace amid celebration and rejoicing. Marduk, the great lord, bestowed on me as my destiny the great magnanimity of one who loves Babylon, and I every day sought him out in awe.
24. My vast troops were marching peaceably in Babylon, and the whole of [Sumer] and Akkad had nothing to fear.
25. I sought the safety of the city of Babylon and all its sanctuaries. As for the population of Babylon [..., w]ho as if without div[ine intention] had endured a yoke not decreed for them,
26. I soothed their weariness; I freed them from their bonds(?). Marduk, the great lord, rejoiced at [my good] deeds,
27. and he pronounced a sweet blessing over me, Cyrus, the king who fears him, and over Cambyses, the son [my] issue, [and over] my all my troops,
28. that we might live happily in his presence, in well-being. At his exalted command, all kings who sit on thrones,
29. from every quarter, from the Upper Sea to the Lower Sea, those who inhabit [remote distric]ts (and) the kings of the land of Amurru who live in tents, all of them,
30. brought their weighty tribute into Shuanna, and

kissed my feet. From [Shuanna] I sent back to their places to the city of Ashur and Susa,

31. Akkad, the land of Eshnunna, the city of Zamban, the city of Meturnu, Der, as far as the border of the land of Guti - the sanctuaries across the river Tigris - whose shrines had earlier become dilapidated,
32. the gods who lived therein, and made permanent sanctuaries for them. I collected together all of their people and returned them to their settlements,
33. and the gods of the land of Sumer and Akkad which Nabonidus – to the fury of the lord of the gods – had brought into Shuanna, at the command of Marduk, the great lord,
34. I returned them unharmed to their cells, in the sanctuaries that make them happy. May all the gods that I returned to their sanctuaries,
35. every day before Bel and Nabu, ask for a long life for me, and mention my good deeds, and say to Marduk, my lord, this: "Cyrus, the king who fears you, and Cambyses his son,
36. may they be the provisioners of our shrines until distant (?) days, and the population of Babylon call blessings on my kingship. I have enabled all the lands to live in peace."
37. Every day I increased by [... ge]ese, two ducks and ten pigeons the [former offerings] of geese, ducks and pigeons.

38. I strove to strengthen the defences of the wall Imgur-Enlil, the great wall of Babylon,
39. and [I completed] the quay of baked brick on the bank of the moat which an earlier king had bu[ilt but not com]pleted its work.
40. [I …… which did not surround the city] outside, which no earlier king had built, his workforce, the levee [from his land, in/int]o Shuanna.
41. [… ....with bitum]en and baked brick I built anew, and [completed] its [work].
42. [… ....] great [doors of cedar wood] with bronze cladding,
43. [and I installed] all their doors, threshold slabs and door fittings with copper parts. [… ....]. I saw within it an inscription of Ashurbanipal, a king who preceded me;
44. [… ....] in its place. May Marduk, the great lord, present to me as a gift a long life and the fullness of age,
45. [a secure throne and an enduring rei]gn, [and may I …... in] your heart forever.

The scribal note from the tablet:

[Written and check]ed [from a…]; (this) tablet (is) of Qishti-Marduk, son of […].

two clay fragments from a Late Babylonian tablet, inscribed with text which duplicates that of the Cyrus Cylinder.

Chapter 7

ترجمۀ متن استوانۀ کورش بزرگ

شاهرخ رزمجو

بخش خاورمیانۀ موزۀ بریتانیا / دانشگاه تهران

۱. [آن هنگام که مر]دوک، پادشاه همۀ آسمان و زمین، [......، ... (که) در ... یَش [... ِ دشمنانش (؟) را] ویران می کند.

۲. [...] با دانایی ِ گسترده (؟)، [... که گو]شه های جهان [را نظاره (؟) می کند]،

۳. [..بزر]گزاده‌اش (=بِلشَزَر)، فرومایه ای به سروری سرزمینش گمارده شد.

۴. [...](نبونئید)[فرمانروایی(؟)سا]ختگی بر آنان گمارد،

۵. نمونه ای (ساختگی) از اِسَگیل سا[خت و ....] برای (شهر) اور و دیگر جایگاه های مقدس [.........]

۶. آیین هایی که شایستۀ آنان (خدایان/پرستشگاه ها) نبود. پیشکشی [هایی ناپاک]..................................... بی پروا [...] هر روز یاوه سرایی می کرد و (به شیوه ای)[اها]نت آمیز

۷. پیشکشی های روزانه را باز داشت. او در [آیین ها دست برد و] .... درون پرستشگاه ها برقرار [کرد]. در دلش به ترس از مردوک–شاه خدایان– پایان [داد].

۸. هر روز به شهرش (=شهر مردوک) بدی روا می داشت [..........

.... همهٔ مردما]نش (=مردمان مردوک) را با یوغی رها نشدنی به نابودی کشاند.

۹. اِنلیل خدایان (=مردوک)، از شِکوهٔ ایشان بسیار خشمگین شد، و [..........................] قلَمرو آنان (را ؟) ....]. خدایانی که درون آنها می زیستند محراب هایشان را رها کردند،

۱۰. خشمگین از اینکه او (=نبوئید) (آنان را) (=خدایان غیر بابلی) به (شهر) شواَنّهَ (=بابل) وارد کرده بود. مردوکِ بلند[پایه، انلیلِ خدایان] برحم آمد. (او) به همهٔ زیستگاه هایی که جایگاه های (مقدس) شان ویران گشته بود

۱۱. و مردم سرزمین سومر و اَکد که همچون کالبد مردگان شده بودند، اندیشه[اش] را بگردانید (و) بر آنان رحم آورد. او همهٔ سرزمین ها را جست و بررسی کرد،

۱۲. شاهی دادگر را جستجو کرد که دلخواهش باشد. او کورش، شاه (شهر) انشان را به دستانش گرفت و او را به نام خواند، (و) شهریاری او را بر همگان به آوای بلند بَرخواند.

۱۳. او (=مردوک) سرزمین گوتی (و) همهٔ سپاهیان مادی را در برابر پاهای او (=کورش) به کرنش درآورد و همهٔ مردمان سرسیاه (=عامهٔ مردم) را که (مردوک) به دستان او (=کورش) سپرده بود،

۱۴. به دادگری و راستی شبانی کرد. مردوک، سرور بزرگ، که پرورندهٔ مردمانش است، به کارهای نیک او (=کورش) و دل راستینش به شادی نگریست

۱۵. (و) او را فرمان داد تا بسوی شهرش (=شهر مردوک)، بابل، برود. او را واداشت (تا) راه (شهر) تینتیر (=بابل) را در پیش گیرد و همچون دوست و همراهی در کنارش گام برداشت.

۱۶. سپاهیان گسترده اش که شمارشان همچون آب یک رودخانه شمردنی نبود، پوشیده در جنگ افزارهایشان در کنارش روان بودند.

۱۷. (مردوک) او (=کورش) را بدون جنگ و نبرد، به درون (شهرِ شواَنّهَ (=بابل) وارد کرد (و) شهرش، بابل را از سختی رهانید.

او (=مردوک) نبونئید، شـاهی را که از او نمی هراسـید، در دستش (=دست کورش) نهاد.

۱۸. همهٔ مردم بابل، تمامی سرزمین سومر و اَکد، بزرگان و فرمانبرداران در برابرش کرنش کردند (و) بر پاهایش بوسه زدند، از پادشاهی او شادمان گشتند (و) چهره هایشان درخشان شد.

۱۹. آنان (مردوک)، سروری را که با یاری اش به مردگان زندگی بخشید (و) آنکه همه را از سختی و دشواری رهانید، شادمانه ستایش کردند و نامش را ستودند.

۲۰. منم کورش، شاه جهان، شاه بزرگ، شاه نیرومند، شاه بابل، شاه سومر و اَکد، شاه چهارگوشهٔ جهان.

۲۱. پسر کمبوجیه، شاه بزرگ، شاه شهر انشان، نوهٔ کورش، شاه بزرگ، شـا[ه شهر] انشان، نوادهٔ چیش پیش، شاه بزرگ، شاه شهر انشان،

۲۲. دودمان جاودانهٔ پادشاهی، که خدایان بِل و نَبو فرمانرواییش را دوست می دارند (و) پاد[شا]هی او را با دلی شاد یاد می کنند. آنگاه که با آشتی به در[ون] بابل در آمدم،

۲۳. جایگاه سروری (خود) را با جشن و شادمانی در کاخ شاهی برپا کردم. مردوک، سرور بزرگ، قلب گشادهٔ کسی که بابل را دوست دارد، همچون سرنوشتم به من [بخشید] (و) من هر روز ترسان در پی نیایش اش بودم.

۲۴. سپاهیان گسترده ام با آرامش درون بابل گام برمی داشتند. نگذاشتم کسی در همهٔ [سومر و] اَکد هراس آفرین باشد.

۲۵. در پیِ امنیت ⌐شهرِ¬ بابل و همهٔ جایگاه های مقدسش بودم. برای مردم بابل [............] که بر خلاف خوا[ست خدایان] یوغی بر آنان نهاده بود که شایسته شان نبود،

۲۶. خستگی هایشان را تسکین دادم (و) از بندها (؟) رهایشان کردم. مردوک، سـرور بزرگ، از رفتار [نیک من] شـادمان گشـت (و)

۲۷. به من کورش، شاهی که از او می ترسد و کمبوجیه پسر تنی[ام و به] همهٔ سپاهیانم،

۲۸. برکتی نیکو ارزانی داشت، تا با آرامش، شادمانه در حضورش باشیم. به [فـرمـان] والایش، همهٔ شـاهانی که بر تخت ها نشسته اند،

۲۹. از هر گوشهٔ (جهان)، از دریای بالا تا دریای پایین، آنانکه در [سرزمین های دور دست] می زیند، (و) شاهان سرزمین اَموِرّو که در چادرها زندگی می کنند، همهٔ آنان،

۳۰. باج سنگینشان را به بابل آوردند و بر پاهایم بوسه زدند. از [شوانّهَ] (=بابل) تا شهر آشور و شوش،

۳۱. اَکد، سرزمین اِشنونهَ، شهر زَمبَن، شهر مِتورنو، دِر، تا مرز گوتی، جایگاه[های مقدس آنسو]ی دجله که از دیرباز محراب هایشان ویران شده بود،

۳۲. خدایانی را که درون آنها ساکن بودند، به جایگاه هایشان بازگرداندم و (آنان را) در جایگاه های ابدی خودشان نهادم. همهٔ مردمانِ آنان (=آن خدایان) را گرد آوردم و به سکونتگاه هایشان بازگرداندم

۳۳. و خدایانِ سرزمین سومر و اَکد را که نبونئید –در میان خشم سرور خدایان– به بابل آورده بود، به فرمان مردوک، سرور بزرگ، به سلامت

۳۴. به جایگاه هایشان بازگرداندم، جایگاهی که دلشادشان می سازد. باشد تا همهٔ خدایانی که به درون نیایشگاه هایشان بازگرداندم،

۳۵. هر روز در برابر (خدایان) بِل و نَبو، روزگاری دراز (=عمری طولانی) برایم خواستار شوند (و) کارهای نیکم را یادآور شوند و به مردوک، سرورم، چنین گویند که "کورش، شاهی که از تو می هراسد و کمبوجیه پسرش

۳۶. ... [... (باشد که) آنان تا روزگاران دراز(؟)، سهمیه دهندگان نیایشگاه هایمان باشند" و (؟)] (باشد که) مردمان بابل شاهیِ مرا ⌐بستایند¬ . من همهٔ سرزمین ها را در صلح (امنیت) نشاندم.

۳۷. .... [غا]ز، دو مرغابی و ده کبوتر، بیشتر از [پیشکشی پیشینِ] غازها و مرغابی ها و کبوترهایی که

۳۸. .... [روزا]نه افزودم. در پی استوار کردن باروِی دیوار ایمگور–انلیل، دیوار بزرگ بابل برآمدم

۳۹. [............................] دیواری از آجر پخته، بر کنارهٔ خندقی که شاهی پیشین ساخته بود، ولی سا[ختش را به پایان نبرده

بود] . . . کار آن را [. . . به پایان بردم.]

۴۰. . . . که [شهر را] از بیرون [در بر نگرفته بود]، که (هیچ) شاهی پیش از من (با) کارگرانِ به بیگاری [گرفته شدهٔ سرزمینش در] بابل نساخته بود.

۴۱. [. . . .] (آن را) [با قیر] و آجر پخته از نو برپا کردم و [ساختش را به پایان رساندم].

۴۲. [. . . . دروازه های بزرگ از چوب های سِدر] با روکش مفرغین. من همهٔ آن درها را با آستانه [ها و قطعات مسی] کار گذاردم.

۴۳. [. . . . کتیبه ای از] آشوربانیپال، شاهی پیش از من، [(بر آن) نو]شته شده بود، [درون آن دید]م.

۴۴. [. . . . در جای خود [نهادم (؟)] . . . . (باشد که) مردوک، سرور بزرگ، همچون هدیه ای به من عطا کند زندگانی دراز، [(و) عمری کامل،]

۴۵. [تختی ایمن و سلطنتی پایدار، و باشد که من . . . . در قلبت تا به] جاودان.

نام کاتب لوحهٔ گلی (مربوط به دو قطعهٔ نو یافته):

[نوشته و تطبیق] شده [از (روی لوحهٔ) . . .]؛ (این) لوحهٔ قیشتی-مردوک، پسرِ [. . .].

سطرهای ۲-۱، ۳۶ و ۴۵-۴۴ به کمک دو قطعه از یک لوحهٔ گلی نویافته در موزهٔ بریتانیا، حاوی نسخه ای دیگر از متن استوانهٔ کورش، بازسازی شده اند.

نقطه چین = شکستگی متن
[ ] = بخش های شکسته و یا بازسازی شده
( ) = توضیحات
(؟) = احتمال ها

List of Contributors

Pierre Briant
Professor of History and Civilization of the Achaemenid World and the Empire of Alexander the Great
Collège de France

Touraj Daryaee
Howard C. Baskerville Professor in the History of Iran and the Persianate World
University of California, Irvine

Irving Finkel
Assistant Keeper, Ancient Mesopotamian Scripts, Languages and Cultures
The British Museum

Ali Mousavi
Curator for the Ancient Iran & the Near East
Los Angeles County Museum of Art

Shahrokh Razmjou
Curator of Ancient Iran & Professor
The British Museum &
The University of Tehran

Matthew W. Stolper
John A. Wilson Professor of Oriental
Studies in the Oriental Institute
University of Chicago

David Stronach

Professor Emeritus, Near Eastern Studies
University of California, Berkeley

Index

C

D

E

F

G

H

I

U

V

W

X

Y

Z